RICOCHET

NEW YORK TIMES BESTSELLING AUTHOR

CHERRY ADAIR

Have fun with Grayson & Hannah

Cheers,

Cherry Adair

RICOCHET

Copyright © 2018 by Cherry Adair – Adair Digital Press

ISBN-13: 978-1937774721
ISBN-10: 1937774724
www.cherryadair.com
shop.cherryadair.com

REVIEW SNIPS

WHIRLPOOL Five Star GOLD. Award-winning Adair has taken readers on thrilling and wild adventures around the globe with an extremely colorful cast of characters. In the sixth and final Cutter Cay novel, she pulls out all the stops with a story that is both emotionally involving and dangerously apocalyptic! Both protagonists, Persephone Case and Finn Gallagher, are immensely engaging and their attraction is a joy to read. Adair also ratchets up the danger and intrigue as an ancient prophecy and those obsessed with it threaten them all. Kudos and thank you for a truly phenomenal ride! ~Jill M. Smith Romantic Times Book Reviews

ABSOLUTE DOUBT. Action, extreme adventure and romance. So much good stuff in this book. A counter-terrorist organization against a sociopath. A hero and heroine who both are honorable, stubborn and loyal and instantly attracted to each other. Totally loved reading this book. It is part of a series, but absolutely can be read alone. ~Fantasy Books

GIDEON. Gritty and action-packed from beginning to end, this is a classic Adair tale, so readers can be sure that the sex is sizzling and the danger relentless! ~Jill M. Smith Romantic Times 4 1/2 * top pick

HUSH Packed with plenty of unexpected plot twists and lots of sexy passion, Cherry's latest testosterone-rich, adrenaline-driven suspense novel is addictively readable. ~Chicago Tribune

HUSH delivers non-stop action, hair raising adventure, and titillating dialogue that will have readers poised on the edge of their seats waiting for what happens next. Ms. Adair has created a memorable couple whose antics are a pleasure to read about. Emotions run high in HUSH, making for an amazing read full of surprising twist and turns. ~ Fresh Fiction

Adair's BLUSH . . . sizzling chemistry adds to the heat of Bayou Cheniere, La., in Adair's knockout contemporary romantic thriller. ~Publishers Weekly starred review

UNDERTOW is full of action and suspense! Cherry Adair did such a great job making the reader feel as if they were part of the experience. I felt like I was right there diving into the water looking for the buried treasure with Zane and Teal. ~Hanging With Bells 4 Bells

WHITE HEAT "...latest in Ms. Adair's T-FLAC series, roars out of the starting gate at a fast gallop and never breaks stride in a thrilling, no-holes-barred roller coaster ride of heart-pulsing suspense and hot romance featuring a delicious, to-die-for hunk..."
"Ms. Adair skillfully weaves an exciting tale of explosive action sprinkled with twisty surprises around a sensual love story laced with gobs of fiery desire. A must for readers who like their romantic suspense hot... and the heroes even hotter!" ~Romance Reader At Heart

HOT ICE is a sure thing! Ms. Adair's characters are well supported by the secondary T-FLAC operatives that assist in the mission. The villain is equally well developed as you come to learn how a man like Jose' Morales became so twisted, that you almost feel sorry for him...almost! Ms. Adair weaves in clever tools and ingenious methods to solve this assignment. There has also been great detail given to the locations/settings, which span many continents. And the ability to bring it all together in a pulse-pounding climax will leave the reader breathless and well satisfied by the time you close this book. ~All About Romance

ICE COLD. Adair continues her wonderfully addictive series featuring the sexy men of T-FLAC with this fast paced and intricately plotted tale of danger, deception, and desire that is perfect for readers who like their romantic suspense adrenaline-rich and sizzlingly sexy. ~ Booklist

WHITE HEAT. "Your mission, should you decide to read it, is to have a few hours adrenaline pumped excitement and sizzling romance with the new T-FLAC suspense by Cherry Adair."

"You'll not want to put this book down as the plot twists come together and explode into a fantastic ending. With the spine-tingling danger, stomach churning suspense, bullets flying from every corner and red-hot romance you get White Heat. Cherry Adair has once again created a heart pounding read with extraordinary characters in extraordinary circumstances that will leave the reader hungering for more. White Heat is an excellent novel and one that I recommend as a keeper." ~ Night Owl Romance

Cutter Cay Series Titles by
CHERRY ADAIR
Undertow
Riptide
Vortex
Stormchaser
Hurricane
Whirlpool

To Max "Mr. Divabetic" Szadek because you are awesome, and support diabetes with flair and dazzle.

I hope showing Hannah running, jumping, being shot at, and having wild monkey sex proves that diabetics can do absolutely anything.

Smooches
Cherry

ONE

Calm seas and a dark moon.

A perfect night for fishing.

Or hunting tangos off the Ecuadorian coast.

Covered head to toe in black LockOut, eyes obscured by night vision goggles, T-FLAC operative Grayson Burke and his men climbed up thin ropes, like shadowy spiders, from the waterline to the upper railings of the slowly moving Megayacht.

Silently landing the length of all three decks, fifteen T-FLAC operatives melted into the darkness, dispersing like smoke.

No exterior lights shone on the luxurious ship, not even running lights. Despite its size, *Stone's Throw*'s occupants didn't want to attract notice. For good reason.

The intel that three high-ranking ANLF lieutenants were on board was the biggest break the counterterrorists had had in months. The fact that the bad guys were contained on board a ship, in the middle of the South Pacific, gave Gray and his men the advantage.

T-FLAC wanted the number one tango on their watch list— the megalomaniac, elusive, sick-fuck, head of the Abadinista National Liberation Front, known only as Stonefish. No one knew who he was, or what the man looked like, but his reign of terror across South America was legendary, and about to get a hell of a lot worse if he pulled off the coup he was masterminding.

If Stonefish gained Cosio, he'd control in a matter of weeks not just the tiny country, but he'd have a firm toehold in Columbia, Peru and Ecuador. Drugs, extortion, torture, weapons...a long fucking list.

Stonefish was T-FLAC's number one priority, and their number one failure to capture to date.

Grayson's failure.

This was more than a mission for Gray. It was extremely personal. For three years he'd been after the son of a bitch. His own capture, on Stonefish's order, was inexorably tied in his head to the loss of Hannah. No matter how hard he tried to forget one, and concentrate on the other, they couldn't be separated.

This time, fucking up wasn't an option.

A good part of South America would be at war if they didn't find and stop him.

But first, they had to capture his men, and extract whatever intel they needed to find him. By whatever means necessary.

Glock raised, Grayson filled his lungs with the smell of salt air, and the faint hint of cigarette smoke as he landed lightly on deck. "Priority," he reminded the three teams on board, speaking low into his comm as they dropped their lines down into the water. He paused for a split second to be certain they were listening. The directive bore repeating, "Secure Sorenson, Deeks and Mauro. Get the hell outta Dodge ASAP."

"Bravo One. Copy that." Kyatta said softly, with his five-person team from their position on the top deck. Wheelhouse. Disable the chopper.

Morrow responded quietly. "Delta One in position." Second deck. Salon.

Echo Team manned the commandeered trawlers—the best they could find on such short notice—lying in wait, silently riding the swells in the matte-black water, ready to return them to Esmeraldas where transport waited.

Gray's Alpha team; below decks, engine room. Using hand gestures he sent them down from the second deck, covering them as the four men went ahead.

This was a snatch and grab. Little communication was necessary from here on out. Everyone knew where to go, and what to do.

The rank, unwashed stink of a heavy smoker preceded the hulking form of a man. "Hostile coming up on your six," Gray alerted his men. "I got him." Visible through the NVGs, the man strolled across his path to stand at the rail. Bodyguard by his bulk, and doing a piss poor job of guarding anybody's body, including his own.

A flick of a lighter, the flare of a cigarette.

Approaching silently from the rear, Gray jerked the slightly shorter man back against him with the crook of his elbow across the man's throat. Cutting off a gargled yelp of surprise, he dug his forearm hard against the guy's trachea. The cigarette went flying, fading to a small red dot, as he fought to get free.

Gray shoved the man's head back and applied the pressure necessary to crush his trachea. *Too late, fuckwad.* Three seconds. Gray stripped the body of the Jericho 941 semi-automatic, tossed it over the rail, and moved on.

In the middle of nowhere, with cloud cover, and no expectation of visitors, the security on board was lax as his men quickly cleared the decks, ready to go inside and extract their targets. The intel had been last minute. Not exactly his style. He liked to be completely prepared. But this was the closest shot he'd had at Stonefish in fucking years, and he wasn't about to pass it up. Gray had just finished an op in Venezuela with these men, and they worked together well.

They'd been strategically in position to close in before the ship reached land.

"Sit-rep?" Gray asked. As each team leader called in a situation report, he scanned the open deck ahead of him. Clear, but he kept his eyes and ears open. The susurrus of the water lapping against the hull was a faint backdrop to the sibilant sound of voices from inside the nearby salon where all the principals were gathered.

Via his comm he heard the scuffle of feet in the darkness, the occasional grunts of pain quickly snuffed.

An *excellent* night for fishing.

"We have visual." Charged with inserting a fiber optic camera through the sliver of the door opening into the salon from the second deck, Darrach, Delta Two, indicated he was in position to observe the players inside the salon.

"Priority targets?" Gray asked, just as another bodyguard came out a side door. Heavy-set, solid, no neck. They saw each other at the same split second. Surprised as shit, the man fumbled for his side arm. Grayson crouched, slid the Tac 11 combat knife from his ankle holster, and threw it true as he rose.

"Mauro, Sorenson, and Deeks," Darrach confirmed. "Five unidentified, six crew."

Verification that Stonefish's lieutenants were indeed on board, made Gray's smile feral in the darkness as he pulled his knife from the man's chest, then wiped off the blood on the guys shirt. The unidentified extras on board, five men, and a woman, were unknown. Sharply aware of every creak, every shadow around him, he slid the knife back into the sheath. "Eyes on the woman?"

"Negative."

"Top deck?" Grayson asked Charlie Kyatta and his team, tasked with clearing the third deck and wheelhouse, then working their way down. Six minutes and they'd all convene on the salon to throw the net.

"Negative," Kyatta said quietly. "Captain. One crew. Guard on the helipad eliminated. Chopper disabled. Nobody's going anywhere tonight."

"Lower deck clear. Three crewmembers. KIA." Alpha Two, Jerry Grazioso reported. "Headed to engine room."

The Echo team, twiddling their thumbs in the waiting fishing boats were keeping a tally of how many people had boarded the Megayacht, and how many KIA since T-FLAC had joined the party. The only person unaccounted for, so far, was the woman.

Using a skeleton key, Gray slipped through the door his team had secured behind them to deter any unwelcome exists or surprise visitors on their six. "Rechecking cabins. Wait for my order, Bravo."

"Copy that."

Gray secured the door behind him, then started down the beautifully wood paneled corridor to see what vermin he could flush out of hiding.

TWO

From the moment Hannah Endicott stepped on board the luxuriously appointed ship with her best-friend/man-she-was-going-to-murder-when-she-got-him-home, she had a bad, bad feeling. An insects-crawling-all-over-her-skin, heebie-jeebie, sort of feeling.

The men Colton insisted she meet were polite and quite sociable. But she didn't like any of them. There was nothing specific she could put a finger on, and it wasn't just her annoyance at Colton. Even though she was way beyond pissed at him, her fight-or-flight antennae were full on vibrating.

Still, if they could afford a luxury ship like *Stone's Throw*, they must be doing something right as far as business went. But she doubted it was legal.

Investors paying in diamonds? That didn't sound legitimate to her at all.

Her gut feelings, as she'd learned to her detriment, were not infallible. Since she was, at present a captive audience, she'd listen to the rest of their presentation at dinner, and reserve judgment.

She'd had no freaking idea, when she reluctantly agreed to meet her friend's business partners for dinner on board, that the multi-gazillion dollar, floating mansion would actually set *sail*. Another damned ride Colton was taking her on whether Hannah liked it or not. For a woman who hated confrontation, Colton was rapidly teaching her that even she had her limits.

She liked knowing what to expect, and preparing for it. She'd been that way her entire life. She wasn't prepared for this. Not in any shape or damn-well-frigging form.

She'd dressed for the flight to Ecuador—*not* a place on her Bucket List. Her favorite jeans, because they were comfortable to travel in, a tucked in men's-style white cotton shirt, and flats so she could run, if necessary, in the concourse. Her purse, a compact tote for this last minute, short trip, was stuffed with two days' worth of clothes, her insulin and a few basic toiletries. That was it. Nothing that fit the glam of this floating palace.

The plan was to get back the money. Fly home.

Dealing with loose diamonds was not something she'd anticipated.

Hannah wasn't a violent woman, but she wanted to grab her friend by his perfectly styled blonde hair, and bash his head against something hard. For a long time. Colton had made a succession of incredibly stupid investments over the years, but she was afraid this one, with these people, made all the others pale into insignificance.

There wasn't a damn thing she could do until they reached the island. Come morning, she wasn't taking no for an answer. In the mean-freaking-time, the ship was in the middle of the South Pacific and all she could do was suck it up, and try not to add homicide to her skill set.

The Captain had informed her while they had cocktails on deck that they were currently between the coast of Ecuador and the Galapagos Islands. A hell of a long way to swim lugging a briefcase of diamonds.

Drying her hands in the luxuriously appointed bathroom, Hannah gave herself a cursory glance in the mirror as she brushed her blunt cut, shoulder-length streaky honey-blonde hair, then wiped a smudge of mascara from under her eye. Applying a little blush to her pale face, she considered her repairs done. No one here she had to impress. She'd leave that to Colton.

She might look like a pushover, but she was far from it. Under her slender frame, and blue eyes, beat the heart of a lion, and she refused to take any bullshit. From Colton or anyone else for that matter. *"Not anymore,"* she added ruefully under her breath.

After her mother's divorce when Hannah was two, they'd moved in next door to thrice divorced Michelle Wickham and her two boys. The women had worked together as flight attendants at the time, and years later had parlayed their love of travel into a small, thriving antiques business in Chicago, a few blocks off The Miracle Mile.

The kids, Colton, Grayson and herself had run tame between the two houses. Nicknamed GQ for how Colton dressed, even when he was small; Tinkerbelle, because Grayson always said she looked like a delicate fairy; and Pumice, the name she'd bestowed on Grayson because of his name, coupled with the color of his eyes, and secretly, because he was always so serious, and gruff, even as a kid. The silly childhood names had stuck.

The Moms disciplined and loved all three equally. Colton and Hannah were the same age, their birthdays days apart, which bonded them quickly. They'd become best friends. Grayson, four years older and wiser, was fascinating because he seemed to have dark and dangerous secrets. Unfortunately for Hannah, that just made him even more appealing.

Secrecy wasn't nearly as enticing as an adult. Hannah, always wanted to see the good in people, especially the people she loved, but she had come to realize that Grayson was one of the bad guys. Disappearing for months on end—once an entire year went by before they saw him—he always returned without a word of explanation.

Always fit and strong, he'd turned into a hardbody.

She straightened her spine. The last person she should be thinking about right now was Grayson and his hard body. She had enough on her plate without adding that toxicity to the acid already churning in her stomach.

She rubbed her upper arms through the thin cotton of her shirt. The enormous bathroom, with miles of chocolate-colored marble, teak, and glass, was damn cold. Or maybe it was her nerves. Pissed and also scared, she headed back to the bedroom, surprised smoke and flames weren't rising from the top of her head to keep her warm.

It had taken her most of her life to realize that she was enabling Colton. "Water under the bridge." Great, now she was talking to herself.

She'd told him the last time that she was done with him helping himself to money that didn't belong to him. She'd meant every damn word, and every threat. She didn't give a flip how she accomplished it, but she wasn't leaving South America without the Moms money, which Colton was using as his buy in for this "Amazing, chance of a lifetime" investment. The money now inconveniently converted to diamonds.

How and when had he acquired the knowledge to convert cash into diamonds? Certainly not at the Life Insurance company where he worked. The little shit had taken their Mothers' life savings while they were in Asia, and hied his ass off to Ecuador. Without a thought for the consequences of his actions. Hannah in hot pursuit.

If she didn't have the money when they returned to shore, she was going to press charges this time and have his sartorial ass thrown in jail.

A South American jail. No more enabling, no more empathy. No more excuses. She was sick and tired of being self-sacrificing. If nothing else, this last stunt of Colton's made her seriously rethink the choices she'd made so that everyone she loved would be happy. What she had given up for everyone around her.

A gifted musician in college, she'd had aspirations of being a concert cellist, of performing on the stages of the largest concert halls in the world. But her mother had needed her help getting the business up and running.

So instead of playing her beloved cello on a stage, she managed Provenance Inc. while the Moms played across Europe on their perpetual buying trips. They hadn't asked, she'd offered. But a year had turned into six. They hadn't taken advantage of her, Hannah knew that. She was a pleaser. It never occurred to her to say no. That was going to change when she got back home. Maybe she'd have "NO" tattooed on her arm as a constant reminder.

Chewing the corner of her lip, she got out the pouch holding her insulin pen and needles from her tote. Yesterday she was rehearsing what she'd say to the Mom's when they returned home in a couple of weeks from this latest buying trip. They didn't need a store front to travel. Between them they had enough money to lead a comfortable, and trip filled life. They could sell Provenance Inc. and she could finally have her own life.

Except that when she'd checked, there was no money. At freaking *all*. One call to the family travel agent, and she'd followed Colton to Ecuador, prepared to be gone from the store for a day, two at the most. Twenty-four hours more than she anticipated needing to knock sense into her friend.

Get the money back. Fly home.

But now that she'd met the men Colton was dealing with, now that she'd seen the obvious wealth, and the slew of no-neck-bodyguard types all carrying enormous guns- "I have no damned idea how the hell I'm going to pull this one off."

The other two investors had each produced a pouch of uncut diamonds as well. There was zero chance of her taking the pouch Colton had handed over under the watchful and vigilant eyes of the businessmen, and their dozen bodyguards in the salon without being caught.

Sick to her stomach at the thought of losing everything the Moms had worked for their entire lives, Hannah prepped her dose on auto-pilot.

As a type one diabetic, she'd been injecting herself since she was old enough to do it on her own. Grayson had been the one to patiently read every scrap of information her mom had brought home from the doctor's office. He was the one to talk her down from freaking out at the thought of injecting herself. He'd calmly and efficiently administered the first, then stood with her as she'd done the next and the next, until she had the hang of it. Grayson was many things, but the man had the patience of a saint.

Hannah still hated him.

And she refused to think about Grayson when she had much bigger fish to fry at the moment. She didn't care how impressive the plans for the resort were, or how much the projected earnings were, the Moms' retirement was not, under any circumstances, going to be part of it.

Ejecting a couple of drops of insulin into the air to remove bubbles, she dialed in the appropriate dose by rote. Whoever these men were, she, Colton and the other investors, were pretty much hostages as the slow moving *Stone's Throw* sailed toward the island where the resort was under construction.

When had her friendship with the man she thought of as a brother, turned into her being his freaking nanny? She'd never felt sisterly toward Grayson. It was Gray who'd given her her first kiss, Grayson who'd been her first lover. The fact that she was still trying not to be in love with him after what he'd done had nothing—okay, it had everything to do with trying to rectify the biggest mistake of her life.

She knew better than to waste time thinking about him. Especially now.

Untucking and lifting her shirt, Hannah pinched a fold of skin at her waist and administered her shot. A loud thump on the door startled her, causing her to jerk her hand. The pen dropped to the floor, then rolled under the edge of the bed skirt.

Damn. Hannah dropped to her knees to find it. "Some-"one's in here!

"Savrov spoke my name." The male voice, American, and very, very angry, was right on the other side of the cabin door while she was in the downward dog position. "Get rid of him."

Not moving an eyelash, Hannah held her breath, waiting for them to keep moving.

A second man, sounding younger and Latin American, asked, "Permanently?"

Something cold and slithery prickled her skin. What did *that* mean?

The first guy didn't say anything for a few seconds. Had he walked away after giving the order? Hannah almost let out the breath she held. "Is the device set?"

Heart lodged in her throat, and pulse thumping uncomfortably she remained on the floor, too scared to move and alert them to her presence. Who *were* these people?

"As you instructed," the younger man said, deferentially. "Exactly thirty minutes, eighteen seconds from now."

"Excellent. I'll bring the others up to the helipad in three minutes. Be ready to take off immediately. Before anyone notices we're missing. I want to be out on open water to watch the show."

What show? Hannah mouthed, afraid she knew the answer. Had she seen too many Bourne and Die Hard movies? Maybe they were talking about something completely different than killing someone, stealing the diamonds, and blowing up their fancy ship as they flew off into the sunset?

Or maybe that's exactly what they were saying.

"What about the crew?"

"What about them?" The American said coldly. That sounded ominous. "Are you offering to be part of the fireworks?"

Hannah's stomach lurched with dread. What the hell? She missed the mumbled response as their footfalls disappeared down the corridor. What had the two men been doing below decks? Looking for her? Setting a bomb? Either thought sent an icy chill across her skin.

Her heart knocked triple time. Colton, plus diamonds, plus the hair on the back of her neck lifting after hours of having a 'bad feeling'? Whoever these men were, Hannah's gut told her in thirty minutes, and however many seconds, the ship was going to blow up with herself and GQ on board.

Not good. Not good at all.

THREE

G rayson entered the well-lit, gleaming mahogany paneled corridor where the cabins were situated. Two men, twenty yards ahead, one in the white crew uniform, the other a salt-and-pepper-haired guy in jeans, dark shirt, a handgun tucked in the small of his back. The *Stone's Throw*, pirated half a world away, had been fully crewed. Those same people were still on board, but it was unlikely the hapless crew knew anything useful about Stonefish.

Collateral damage was inevitable.

With a silenced pop, Grayson got off one, well-placed shot, hitting the jean-clad man in the back of the neck just beneath his skull. Half his brain splattered on the mahogany paneling in front of him, dropping like a felled oak part-way up the carpeted stairs. Without hesitation, the crewmember broke into a run, disappearing up the stairs, where the rest of Grayson's team lay in wait. They'd contain him. Done and done.

Using the skeleton key, he systematically checked each cabin, finding the woman in the second to last room, at the far end of the hall from the stairs where the man had disappeared. Long legs, and a shapely, jean-clad ass was all he could see of her. He wasn't sure if she was dead, passed out, or taking a nap on the floor half under the bed.

Soundlessly crossing the room, Grayson gave her ankle an economical yank, pulling her free of the bed hangings, and hauled her to her feet in one smooth move. Pressing her back against his chest, he palmed her mouth well before the scream he felt vibrating in her chest erupted.

He'd killed women in the line of duty, but he hated doing it. A pop to the back of the skull, like the man out in the corridor, and it would be over. In his line of work he didn't have time to linger or get soft.

She, however *was* soft. Soft and fragrant and madder than hell as she fought him for all she was worth. But since his arms were banded over hers, and he was holding her tightly against him, she was pretty ineffective. His head jerked back as she tried to head-butt him, harmless, except that her blossom-scented, honey-blonde hair, lashed across his cheek.

Grayson's senses filled with a unique, scent-induced memory, and a struggling woman whose body felt exactly like Hannah's. His momentary distraction was all she needed to twist out of his hold, and come at him with her full body weight.

Fuckit.

Grayson felt as though he'd just taken a shot to the chest.

He hoped his mind was playing tricks on him, because God only knew he'd had this particular fantasy before. A time or two...or a thousand.

He reached out, grabbing her, and twisted so he landed on top of her on the bed, clamping both slender wrists in one hand over her head. He used his weight to hold her thrashing legs down with his feet bracketing her ankles. Furious blue eyes met his as she bucked beneath him.

Fucking hell. No mistake. "Jesus. Hannah?"

With her honey blonde hair spread in a wild tangle around her head and shoulders, and her breasts pressed against his chest, she looked more perfect than that girl next door. More heart-stoppingly beautiful now than she'd been on that summer night by the lake where he'd taken her virginity, and only slightly less pissed than when he'd returned home to claim her on the anniversary of their wedding day.

Going deadly still, she stared up at him in shock and horror, big blue eyes wide. "Grayson?" she gave a bitter laugh. "Oh, this nightmare just gets better and better." She shoved at his shoulders with both hands. When he didn't budge, she stopped struggling and just lay there, glowering up at him, her soft mouth a flat, angry line.

He considered the two men in the corridor. "Did you come in here alone?"

"Just me and the Chicago Blackhawks." Tone dry, eyes blazing, she held onto whatever deep emotion she was feeling. A new skill. She used to be an open book. He was the one lousy at communicating. Unless they were in bed, He did just fine communicating there.

He could almost feel her anger lashing out like a sharp cat o' nine tails ripping into his flesh, his heart, his brain.

Her chest rose, then fell as she sucked in a calming breath. Her eyes were shockingly blue, and as cold as the tundra. The look was unfamiliar to him, and her fear and disdain made something hot and tight clench inside him.

"For God sake, Pumice, I've been going to the bathroom by myself since I turned three. I came to take my insulin shot before dinner." She looked him over, with a scowl. "Why are you dressed like a giant black sperm?"

Her presence in the middle of this clusterfuck was so out of context he had a hard time wrapping his brain around it. "Were you coerced?" he demanded flatly. "Kidnapped?"

Experience told him that there wasn't anything too improbable, too dangerous, too vile, to be a possibility.

"I might ask you the same damn question. Why are you here, Pumice? Because as we both know, you never do anything that isn't completely self-serving. In that, you and your brother are frigging peas in a pod."

Because his friends and family didn't know he worked for T-FLAC, they figured he was some kind of underworld criminal. It killed Gray, but that's the way it was. He lived with it. And this woman with the soft, sassy mouth whose loving heart had turned to stone between one beat and the next, tied him in knots because he knew, being here, just cemented what she'd thought all along. "Answer the damn question, Hannah." He kept his voice brusque and all business.

"News-flash Grayson Burke. Talk to me in that tone again, and I'll cut off your balls and feed them to you as a little snack." He didn't miss the way the word little was stressed.

He gave her a feral smile. "Hard to do all that when said balls are pressed up tight against you."

"You have to get up sometime," she responded sweetly. "I'll wait."

"No, as history proves, you *don't* wait."

She made an inarticulate sound of anger, and her cheeks flushed. "You decide to follow me halfway around the world to attack me, so you can discuss old news? Worse. Imply that *I* was in the wrong? Go to hell, Gray, just go to hell."

"Answer the damn question. What are you doing here, Hannah?" Grayson repeated grimly. Through his comm he could hear his men gathering outside the salon, ready to burst in. He should be up there with them.

She returned his frown, not looking any happier than he was. Soft breasts pressed against his chest as she sighed. "Colton's upstairs."

"Christ."

Of *course* his brother was involved in this goatfuck. Hannah was always bailing him out of some damned mess.

She didn't move, but the suppressed fury in her voice was like a third party in the room with them. "Get off. You're hurting me."

"If I wanted to hurt you, you wouldn't be speaking right now." Gray inhaled her light citrusy perfume, which still affected him the way it always had. That perfume, and his reaction to her, hadn't changed. At least he was consistent.

This dainty, five-foot-four, feisty fairy of a woman was his Achilles Heel. Always had been, always would be. Her pulse throbbed hard beneath the manacle of his fingers around her wrists. He wanted to touch more than her bare wrists.

One thousand and ninety five days since he'd held her. Dear God, smelling the achingly familiar scent of her skin took his breath. His eyes burned as the ache grew. Smelling her hair, touching her silky skin, seeing her again, after fantasizing, scared the crap out of him. The reality made the memories pale into insignificance.

Despite the dangerous situation, his dick pushed painfully hard against the confining LockOut, and his heart thudded heavily against his rib cage. Hard enough that she must feel it too.

He had to go back to work, he knew he did, but his entire world focused down to the woman beneath him. She had an incredible mouth, soft and beautifully shaped, he remembered how those lips felt all over his body.

Her breath caught, and a tremor rippled through her as she read his intentions quite clearly. "Oh, no you don't! I'm warning you, Pumice. . . " She braced herself, eyes, the vivid blue of forget-me-nots, flashed dangerously.

He studied her generous mouth. The dark length of her eyelashes. The soft, petal-pink of her cheeks. His memory hadn't done her justice. Everything about Hannah was delicate, her slender body, the slim column of her neck, her graceful hands. But there was nothing fragile about her inner strength. She could be stubborn and intractable if she believed she was right, and he knew this encounter could sway either way. After her initial surprise- like a nanosecond after- she was mad as hell.

Still. But when her eyes darkened – like *that*, and her pink tongue made a sexy swipe, he knew he'd won half the battle.

"Do *not* do it!" she warned in a dire voice.

Her warm, intensely female scent, with just a hint of orange blossom, rose up to meet him from the velvety V between the collars of her plain white shirt. He wanted to drink in the smell. Bottle it to save for later. Heart pounding with anticipation, he lowered his head the last inch, covered her mouth with his, brushing her soft lips. Once. Twice.

He made a low sound of desire and need. "This?" he whispered, cupping her flushed cheek in one hand, while holding her wrists firmly over her head with the other. He lowered his mouth over hers, trailing his fingertips over her cheekbone, reacquainting himself with her the feel of her. So soft. Silky. Inhaling deeply, he breathed in the intoxicating scent of the citrus blend soap she'd been using for years.

To Grayson, Hannah epitomized everything good. Everything clean. Every joy and every hope. She'd always been a part of his life. A part of him.

His fingers spread at the base of her throat where her pulse jumped unevenly. His body's visceral response to the mere brushing of their lips was way out of proportion. Hunger, simmering just under the surface for years, erupted in a hot blast of lust impossible to contain.

She attempted to clamp her lips closed against the invasion of his marauding tongue, but Gray wasn't playing fair. He knew that stroking the back of her neck made her melt, knew how to angle his head, so that their mouths seemed to function like parts of a whole. She let him in, her slick tongue dueling with his, hungry for him, just as she'd always been. God. He reveled in her taste—sunshine, love, promise- intensified as he lost himself in her moist, yielding mouth.

Wanting her so bad, he couldn't think straight and he closed his eyes, giving in the driving, need. Tangling his fingers in the silky, fragrant strands of her hair he drove the kiss hotter, deeper.

With the cool silk of her hair brushing his wrist, he cupped the back of her head, angled her head, nipped at her lips. Stroked her tongue with his until her breath hitched and he felt the rapid pulse throbbing behind her ear. Her scent became her taste, oranges, a slick mix of erotic, heady textures.

She fought the restraint of his grip, but Gray didn't let go, even when she growled her annoyance deep in her chest. He felt her hand fist, open, fist again in the manacle of his fingers as she fed off the kiss.

He stroked his open palm down the arching cords of her throat as Hannah sank into the kiss. Shifting his upper body to gain better access, he trailed his hand over the smooth skin beneath the V of her shirt to find her breasts. Sliding his fingers beneath the thin satin of her bra, he cupped one breast as his heart beat triple time at the warm, and familiar weight. Skimming his thumb over her hard nipple, something inside him uncoiled at her automatic response.

His chest ached. His brain ached. His balls fucking ached. He thought he'd never be here again. Been sure of it. Each hard, painful throb of his heart echoed her name. *Hannah. Hannah. Hannah.*

The reality far surpassed the fantasy as he grazed her lips with his teeth, before sweeping inside to explore the hot wet cavern.

She bit his tongue. *Hard.*

FOUR

amn. That hurt!" Gray lifted his head, reluctantly disengaging from the kiss.

Hannah dragged in a deep, shuddering breath. "It was supposed to." She gave him a furious look. Eyes dilated and glittering, she didn't move so much as a muscle, although he knew she wanted to pummel the crap out of him and buck him off her. Preferably into the South Pacific Ocean.

The stain of hot pink flushing her cheeks made her eyes look bluer, more intense. "Get your damned hand off my boob, Pumice. I mean it."

Yeah. He saw that she did. Reluctantly he uncurled his fingers, so happy where they were with the hard peak of her nipple pressing against his palm. He took his time. But he couldn't make a grope last forever.

"You bastard." Hannah thumped his back with both fists. It hadn't taken long to piss her off enough for her to forget restraint. "That was a lousy thing to do."

He wanted her to fight him. Just so he could restrain her and steal another kiss. But Hannah knew him just as well as he knew her. She wasn't going to give him that opening. He gave her the smile he knew annoyed her. "You loved it."

"Which is why it was a lousy thing to do. I have no desire to be kissed by you. Ever. I won't wrestle you, but get the hell off me. We can't lie like this all night, and you don't have the element of surprise to sneak another kiss. Get the hell off me."

Reluctantly Gray rolled off and on his feet, then pulled her up before she could protest him touching her. The brief contact flooded his brain with images of the two of them entwined, of her under him, eyes liquid with love, soft skin flushed and damp from their lovemaking. Of Hannah straddling his hips, her cool blonde hair a private silken cave sheltering them and their love. Her slender hands, so delicate and talented on the strings of a cello, touching every part of his body.

In the darkest nights, when missing Hannah had been an intense, unbearable, painful ache, he would relive the brush of her fingers, followed by the soft skim of her lips all over his body.

Yanking her hand free, she glared at him.

As much as he wanted to hash out the past, fix it, now was not the time, and definitely not the place. Gray rubbed his fist over the deep ache in his chest. Would there ever be a time and place? "There isn't time for niceties, Tink, cut to the chase. What's GQ involved in now?"

"You have the gall to ask me that? Or anything else for that matter, when the last thing you said to me, was, 'See you next week, Tink.' That was three years ago."

"I came." He'd left the hospital AMA the moment he could stand for longer than thirty seconds without passing out, the ring box in his pocket. Then he'd seen her kissing some guy at the store as if she was mining for his goddamned tonsils. His mother had casually mentioned at dinner that night that Hannah had found a wonderful boyfriend.

The pain in his chest had been so excruciating, he hadn't felt his stitches tearing. He'd left the house before Hannah came home next door, before he made a fool of himself, and because he couldn't hide the spread of blood on his shirt.

Fuck it. The image of Hannah lifting a wedding veil for her husband's kiss made him want to punch the wall. Since he was already fucked, he'd gone back to work.

"You missed your own damn wedding. Without a call. A note. A damn carrier pigeon!" she said, voice flat, eyes cold.

"You refused to talk to me."

"A year late? Did you really think you could just show up like that, out of the blue, and I'd *want* to listen to anything you had to say? I'd moved on Gray. I was- *am*- done with you. I really am."

None of them had forgiven him, and Hannah, after a disgusted look, had refused any communications.

Just because he understood the pain he'd caused her, understood seeing him again was reconstituting that pain, didn't mean it hurt him any less.

He'd cut off his left ball not to hurt her. Brushing a strand of her pale hair out of eyes shooting death rays up at him. Seeing that unfamiliar look made his chest feel exactly the way it did when a bullet struck his LockOut. Dull, throbbing fucking pain. "You hair's shorter."

"You're joking, right?" Slapping his hand away, she shot him a disbelieving look. "You're in the wrong place, at the wrong damned time, and you want to talk about my hair? You've come to steal the frigging diamonds, haven't you? Damn it, Grayson. I'm out of the rescuing business. All I came to do is get Colton's share back. Whatever you're here to do, whatever your brother is involved in, count me out."

25

Grayson had no damned idea what diamonds she was talking about. His mind went there. Diamonds to pay for the weapons on order for the coup? Jesus. Getting their hands on the money would certainly delay Stonefish's plans. Long enough to expose where he was?

"Go ahead and steal the rest, but Colton's share belongs to *me*, and I'm not leaving without them."

He made a frustrated, inarticulate sound. "Christ, for once can't you just take my word for it—I'm the good guy, Tink."

"When did that happen?" she asked sarcastically. "Were you rehabilitated during your incarceration?"

His jaw clenched. "I've never been in jail." Not jail. But he'd been held prisoner for a few months in a hellhole, where all that had sustained him were his fist, his imagination and memories of Hannah.

He'd been captured by the very man he was trying to capture. Just a month before he was supposed to return to marry her. Tortured, and held for three months, then rescued by a T-FLAC exfil team. Hospitalized, it had taken another six months before he was capable of checking himself out of the hospital, and onto a plane.

Too fucking late.

Her blue glare was molten. "I'll call your parole officer to confirm that."

Grayson had spent half his life bailing his younger brother out of one scrape after another, years lusting after his brother's best friend, and now his teeth clenched so hard he was sure the enamel was cracking.

"I didn't even know Colton was involved. I'm not here for *either* of you, believe me." Jesus fuck. Every time his brother got some wild investment, harebrained opportunity, he went to the Moms and used good looks and charm to con them out of a huge sum. They'd finally stopped enabling him and told him no more. So much for that vow. "How much did he take this time?"

"All of it," she said bitterly. "He used his Power of Attorney to access- None of your damn business. I'm dealing with him. I can't image you'd care enough to follow me here."

"If I'd known you weren't safely at home in Chicago minding the store, or had an inkling where you were, hell yes, I would have. However, I had no idea either of you were here. And I wish to hell you weren't." In fact, he wished them both a thousand miles away.

"Sorry to inconvenience you."

A muscle in his jaw jerked, as, beyond the closed door, he heard the faint pops of gunfire. "You have no idea."

Gray knew what was going on all around them. Anyone coming between his men and the three principals was being eliminated. The body count would be high. Shit. What a clusterfuck.

His men were talking in shorthand in his ear. He should be up on deck with them, securing the prisoners for transportation. But with their communication, he also heard gunshots, running feet, shouts. Since he dared not risk leaving Hannah anywhere onboard unattended while he did his thing, his only choice was to stay glued to her side until he could get her- and GQ- onto one of the waiting trawlers.

He activated his comm. "Let me know when everyone's secure. I have the woman with me. My idiotic brother is here, too. Tall, blond. Looks like a movie star. Colton. Don't scuff up his designer outfit. Bring him downstairs. Second cabin on the left."

"The *woman*?" Hannah gave him a hostile look, as he disconnected. "Lovely. So you're not alone in this little venture, you brought thugs? Are you going to te-"

He pressed a finger to her soft lips to silence her as his headset beeped discreetly in his ear. "Package secure." Grazioso told him. "On our way."

Her expression tightened and she slapped his hand away from her face.

"Sit-rep?" Keeping an eye on her, Gray listened to his teams as they reported in. They had everyone in the salon, ready for departure. "Take the packages and start processing. I'll be right behind you."

While he talked, Hannah dropped to her knees, giving him a nice view of her jean-clad ass as she foraged under the bed, then rose to stand several feet further away, her insulin pen in her hand. A timely reminder of just how damned inconvenient—how fucking dangerous—this situation had become. Not just for a civilian, but this delicate, beautiful, sprite of a civilian. Hannah had type one diabetes.

How many insulin pens did she have with her? She was nothing if not practical. If she'd expected to be here for a day or two, she would've brought enough for two weeks. Or had this little voyage to nowhere been a surprise? In which case, not enough. "How much insulin did you bring with you?"

"Enough," she told him flatly. Her snapping eyes said 'what I do, and how I do it, are none of your fucking business.'

She wasn't his to worry about. His stomach knotted. He had to let it go.

"Does what you're doing here have anything to do with Colton's new business partners? Because, just so you know, they insisted that he and the other two guys pay their share in loose diamonds. Which just adds another layer of wtf to this whole situation."

What the fuck was about right. "Diamonds can't be traced. Or not easily anyway. And at that, the trail would lead to my idiotic brother and the other two morons who fell for this elaborate scam. These aren't businessmen, and trust me, there's no investment other than a dozen rocket launchers, crates of South African Amscor BXP submachine guns, and PPS43's from Russia. These guys are Abadinista National Liberation Front, and they're about to stage a coup that, if not stopped, will change the face of South America forever."

"Terrorists, Hannah," he said, voice stone cold. "The diamonds are to fund a massive arms deal the ANLF has brokered, and the weapons they've been amassing for six months."

"They told Colton they're building a fancy resort on a private island." She chewed her lower lip, mulling over what he'd said. Grayson could practically hear the gears in her brain clacking.

"While I've already stated my disapproval—vehemently—the model of the complex is upstairs in the salon," she admitted coolly, chin up, eyes not quite so sure. "As much as I don't like or trust them, I have to admit from what I've seen of the plans, their complex resort looks spectacular. Maybe this time GQ will surprise us all."

Grayson cocked a disbelieving brow. "Jesus, Hannah. Did you drink the Kool-Aid?"

FIVE

Hannah kept her game face on. "I can do without the sarcasm," she lifted her chin, keeping her gaze rock steady, as her tummy fluttered with unease.

Grayson smelled of the ocean. Not soap, or cologne. Just sexy, salty potent male. His dark hair, short-cropped, and as shiny as a seal's pelt, clung to his well-shaped head. The sheen of dark beard stubble reminded her of nights in his bed, and the morning after when he'd left pink marks all over her. That soft prickle against her skin excited her, and she'd begged him never to shave again.

His face looked leaner than the last time she'd seen him. Two years ago, and for all of ninety seconds before she turned her back and walked away. Gray eyes, which used to look gentle and loving, were as cold as fog.

A thin white scar at the corner of his mouth, and another on his tanned forehead showed he'd been in trouble before.

He'd aged. Looked harder.

He was a dangerous stranger now.

She had a flash of memory of her pale fingers stroking down the crisp hair on his broad chest, her mouth trailing down the smooth skin of his abs. He was just-damn it- he was too male. Too damned appealing for his own good. And now he was just irritating as hell.

"Of course I don't buy everything they're selling up there. I'm not the idiot," she said with conflicting emotions. Everything Grayson was telling her resonated. Now she didn't know if she should trust him or not. When the chips were down—and God only knew they were—would Grayson help? Or would he stick to his nefarious agenda? Because, by the look of him he'd come ready for a fight, and she had no idea whose side he was on.

This whole situation was scary as hell.

That she could debate this with a straight face just showed Hannah she still had an ounce of loyalty left for her friend. And that she was a great freaking actress, because as Gray spoke, she realized what he said made perfect sense, and that was the vibe she'd been picking up all along.

"Where did they say they were taking you?" his voice was hard. Everything about him was hard. His pumice-gray eyes were shrewd and penetrating, missing nothing as he watched her like a wolf watched a fox.

She could do without that freaking patronizing tone of voice, but Hannah met his gaze unwaveringly. "Apparently to see the progress of construction on their private island." Hating him, she smiled sweetly, because whatever Grayson's agenda here, and God only knew that could be anything, she had to get Colton and herself off the ship as quickly as possible. How, she wasn't sure. But it would come to her.

Soon, she hoped.

His brow went up again. Irritating man. "Visiting a construction site? At eight at night, in the pitch dark?"

Nobody could cock an eyebrow like Grayson Burke. It said many things, most of them rude and insulting. She'd been trying to master the skill for years.

"Don't be an ass." She wanted to stay angry, she wanted to maintain the same level of hurt and disappointment, because if she started believing anything he said right now, it could be very, very dangerous. A lot of things could change in three years. She'd known him once, but she didn't know this inscrutable, dangerous, enigma at all. "We're seeing it in the morning." *Unless we're all dead by then.*

"There's not a damn thing on that island but an old boathouse," Grayson said tightly. "The investors have been duped. The ANLF will take the stones and disappear. And more than likely, they'll kill the 'investors' before they hightail it off the ship. Didn't you find it suspicious that GQ had to pay in diamonds?"

"I didn't know about the form of payment until he showed me as we were boarding. He gave the pouch to some muscle-bound guy with a gun, a thick Spanish accent, dyed black hair, and a scowl." She didn't want to cry wolf, but perhaps now was a good time to mention the conversation she'd overheard.

Unless Grayson was in on whatever was going on? His appearance here and now was way too freaking convenient as far as Hannah was concerned.

Torn, she tried to picture the layout of the ship, and if she'd seen any lifeboats. There must be some on a ship this size...

Okay. Hannah's brain was in overdrive, *Let's just say, there really is a bomb. Let's say I have less than thirty minutes to find Colton, figure out how to get a lifeboat into the water—let's just go ahead and say...The situation looks frigging hopeless.*

God. Used to being the person everyone looked to for solutions, this was going to be a dramatic and permanent fail.

"Ignado Mauro. The head guy's number two lieutenant. He's the one we came for. Did you see what they did with the diamonds?"

"They're on the table next to the 3-D model of the resort. Or they were fifteen minutes ago when I came down here."

"Payment is diamonds, near model," he told someone. Then addressed her. "My men will find them."

"Who are you talking to?"

"My men."

"Great." Okay. *More* men. Two groups to evade now. Colton's friends with their neck-less bodyguards, and Grayson with his "men". How many? "Make sure they hold onto a third of them. I'm taking those home with me." Pushing her hair off her face, she gave Grayson an up and down look. As much as she hated him, if he was the last person she saw before she died, she wanted to be in his arms, not talking about Colton. *Ugh*. Where had that thought come from? Shaking her head slightly, she tried to think clearly, "Your men, huh?"

He had no right to look so good. He should be ravaged with shame, and bowed with unhappiness. Instead he looked tanned and handsome, and ridiculously buff in the thing he was wearing which looked like a skintight wetsuit. The matte black defined his broad shoulders, the ridges of his abs, and his strong arms and legs. Her eyes dropped to his groin, where his package was tucked away, the large bulge flattened behind a hard protective covering which she'd felt when he was on top of her.

Seeing that bulge, brought a visceral muscle memory to her body, of his narrow hips pounding against her as he made love to her. They hadn't been able to keep their hands off each other-

Maybe the men she'd overheard hadn't meant a *bomb*. Maybe they'd been talking about.... What else could they *possibly* have meant? Good guy or bad guy, this was still Grayson. And while Hannah sure as shit didn't trust him with her heart, she did trust him to protect her when the chips were down. And how much more could chips be down than being within yards of a bomb?

"But more importantly-"

"Call it in to the Peruvian authorities, and we'll leave it for them to deal with. Five." Gray, still talking to someone else, looked up to catch Hannah watching him. "Did you take your insulin?"

She nodded. Over the shock of seeing him in the last place she expected to see him, Hannah's synapses started firing. None of that was important now. "Gray. Listen to me. There's a-"

The door slammed open and Colton burst in. "Hannah, the ship is crawling with terrorists—Grayson?" If not for the Botox, he'd be frowning. "What the fuck?" Not a blonde hair out of place, his summer white designer suit immaculate, the body hugging black, silk t-shirt underneath molded to his flat stomach, Colton looked like a GQ cover model in all his sartorial splendor.

Gray grabbed his brother by the upper arm and jerked him further into the room, which suddenly felt crowded as a man dressed as Gray was, and also carrying a large black gun, followed behind Colton and shut the door.

Clearly Grayson was controlling the urge to do violence to his younger brother. Hannah knew how he felt. That was probably the one thing they still had in common. She curled her short nails into her palms as she moved out of the way. She was so letting him do his thing.

Grayson shook him. "What the *fuck* are you doing here, Colton?"

His brother struggled uselessly in his grip. "Goddamn it, Grayson! What are *you* doing here? Are you hijacking the ship?" he paused, his eyes going from his older brother's face, to the gun he was suddenly holding, to the pushed back cowl and black outfit.

Realization dawned, and he stepped back. "Oh, shit! You came to steal the diamonds, didn't you? You can't!" Colton spluttered furiously. "The diamonds are my share, my *investment*, of the construction costs. Don't even *think* about fucking with my business. Jesus. Didn't you see? The ship's crawling with bodyguards. You can't possibly get away with this!"

"I don't give a shit about diamonds, only that they don't get into the wrong hands. We're here for Deeks, Sorenson and Mauro. They work for Stonefish. Is the name familiar?" Gray demanded, eyes and voice flat, uncompromising. Hannah felt the hair on the back of her neck rise. His stance, feet spread, gun at his side, made her damn glad he wasn't aiming that tightly leashed anger at her.

"Stonefish? What the hell is that?" Colton's face grew flushed. Anyone else seeing him with this irate, and blustering would think he was pissed. But Hannah knew her friend better. His belligerent tone of voice set her teeth on edge.

Denial. Panic. Realization. Followed by fear.

It was bad enough that she was here to beat the crap out of him for stealing from the Moms. *Again.* But now his big brother was here, too. He knew he was screwed. Like any thief, he felt guilty for getting *caught*. He hated being called out. Especially in front of witnesses. "I can assure you, the Ecuadorian authorities are going to have a field day," he snarled with false bravado. "You'll be in jail for a long, long time. This time you've gone too far, Grayson. This is going to kill the Moms and you know it."

"The real question here is, what the fuck are you doing with a bunch of terrorists, asshole? You knew Hannah would hightail it after you to get the Moms' money back. Did you give her safety a nanosecond's thought? You're in way over your head, and you're too stupid to know it. And for your information, your friends are the ones who are the terrorists, and they already hijacked this ship."

"I'm a counterterrorist operative with T-FLAC. We're here to bring these assholes to justice. You and Hannah are in the wrong fucking place, at the wrong fucking time."

A counterterrorist operative? She felt a sudden glimmer of hope as all the words dropped into all the right slots in her brain. Her heart skipped several, uneven beats.

Dear God. This explained his long absences, his refusal to discuss what he did for a living for all these years. But if it was his job that had kept him away, why hadn't he just *told* her? Why leave her in the dark? Not just herself, but his mother and brother?

"What are you trying to pull?" Colton railed. "They're not terrorists, they're international businessmen, and I bet they've dealt with punks like you all over the world. Your people may have overpowered them, now. But I'm sure there'll be more security people once we reach the island. You'll never get away with this."

Grayson let out a hard breath. "Wanna know what you'll find on that island? A fifty-year-old boathouse, trees and rocks. Those guys are, among other things, weapons brokers, dickwad. Weapons. Brokers. *Terrorists*."

Colton glared at his brother. "I already told Hannah, and this is all either of you need to fucking know. I'll pay the money back four-fold in less than a year."

"You'll forgive me if I don't want to rehash how many times I've heard that bullshit, GQ." Hannah interrupted furiously. "I told you for the last time. I am done. You've stolen from the Moms for the last frigging time. I'm not leaving until I have every dime of their money back where it belongs waiting for them when they get home from their buying trip. And I'd listen to Grayson right now, because I believe him."

"Shit." Raking his fingers through his immaculate sandy-blonde hair, Colton gave a haunted look from Hannah and back to his brother. "We're building a three thousand, six hundred room resort. Go take a look at the 3-D model and the architectural drawing." He jerked a thumb up at the ceiling. "I'm staking the three bars-" Realizing he wasn't getting any points right now, his shoulders slumped.

"Fucking hell. I'm in way over my head with this one, aren't I?" he admitted, his usually booming voice subdued. Dropping down on the foot of the bed, he looked helplessly from Hannah to Gray. "What the fuck do I do now?"

SIX

Typical Colton. He was all bluff and bravado until he was called out. Then he needed help cleaning up his mess. Hannah was suddenly grateful Grayson was there.

His older brother treated him with a grim look, and a weighted pause. "What did they do with the diamonds?"

Colton shrugged in a too casual gesture that made Hannah want to slap him. Controlling the urge took a great deal of effort. "No idea," he said, surely and defensive. "I handed my pouch to two bodyguards when we boarded. That was the last I saw it."

Grayson ran his hand over his short hair as he looked beyond Colton to the other man. "Any sign of them?"

"Negative."

"Check with the others."

The other man stepped out of the door, and spoke indistinctly. While he was gone, Grayson let the silence fill the room unbearably. Colton swiped a trickle of sweat off his temple with fingertips that shook.

The man returned to the room. "Nobody's seen them. We're looking."

"I suggest you take this opportunity to redeem yourself," he told his brother, voice hard and cold, "Any idea where they took the stones?".

Sweat gleamed on Colton's forehead. Good. He was scared. As he should be. "I might," he said reluctantly. How she'd not noticed that sulky expression over the years was a mystery to Hannah. What she'd loved about him was his uncomplicated charm, his zest for life. Until he'd started using the Moms' money for various sure fire investments. Then the bloom had started fading from the rose. Now that she thought about it, her friendship with Colton had disintegrated at the same time as her non-wedding.

"Go with him." Grayson addressed the other man, who immediately grabbed a protesting Colton by the upper arm. "Don't let him get any holes in him. I'm not done reaming him a new one, yet. Go." The door had barely closed, and he turned to Hannah. "Get your stuff. We're leaving."

She put her hand on his forearm without thinking. The black garment he wore felt odd, now that she had a moment to process it, but that wasn't what she was having a visceral reaction to. She hadn't touched him, willingly anyway, in three years. A lifetime. Her fingers curled around his arm, and she shuddered with the need to fling herself against his chest and have him hold her tightly.

Instead, she tucked her fingertips into the front pockets of her jeans. "There's a bomb on board," she said calmly, while her heart pounded, and her palms slicked with nervous sweat.

"A bomb?" Without any pause between her words and his actions, Grayson propelled her out into the corridor. He had a large black gun in one hand, and her upper arm in a merciless grip in the other. She'd never guess that a man his size could move so quickly. She had to practically run to keep up.

"Explosive on board. Find it-" He looked at Hannah she tried to keep up with his longer strides. "Detonation?"

She was more terrified now that Gray believed her, than five minutes ago when she'd been trying to talk herself out of making sense of the conversation. "They said thirty minutes. But that was—"

"Don't look down." Gray picked her up bodily to put her several steps beyond a man, sprawled out across the foot of the stairs, his head splattered on the wall nearby. The display of graphic violence made bile rose in the back of her throat as her feet touched the stair above him. She slapped a hand on the wall to keep her balance even though Grayson's hand was still holding onto her.

"Less than twenty. Go!" He straddled the dead man with his long legs, and kept her moving with a lethal grip on her upper arm as he propelled her up the stairs. Through the door, and into the salon which looked like a war zone. Hannah's shoes crunched on broken glass and shards of china. It wasn't easy keeping up with Grayson's long strides.

The beautifully rendered three dimensional model was smashed to smithereens on and around the table, there was a huge hole in one of the picture windows, and the room smelled pungently of the liquor spilled on the floor near the bar.

Her arm was almost wrenched from the socket as she stumbled over bits of plastic and balsa wood strewn in their path. Crying out she dropped to one knee, hands bracing her fall.

"Keep moving, honey. Come on." Grayson hauled her up like a sack of feed. They burst through the door onto the deck where men were securing the crew who all protested loudly in various languages.

The cool air smelled really awful, as Grayson pulled her alongside him and she stumbled her way between the bodies littering the deck, she saw, with horror, why. He wore a grim expression, and kept the gun at ready in his other hand. Since the only men standing seemed to be his, and other than the contained crew, everyone else was apparently dead, the gun seemed redundant.

Her steps slowed in horror. The scene was surreal. In the light streaming from the open doors, men dressed in black moved silently and with purpose as they headed toward the back of the ship. The throb of engines came from below. She held her breath from the smell of death, and the fear of what else could come out of the enveloping darkness surrounding the small island of light that was the deserted Megayacht.

The fact that Grayson believed her about the bomb, without concrete confirmation frightened her more than her imagination had . Wrapping one strong arm around her waist when she faltered, forced her to run to keep up with his long strides. Her tote—with her wallet, passport, all her money, and insulin—was downstairs.

"Behind me," Gray shouted, suiting action to words as he slung her around his back as two figures leapt out of the darkness. Two burst of light and two loud shots sounded before Hannah even knew what was happening.

"Come on." Gray pulled her back to his side. "Don't look. Move it."

Ice cold from head to toe, Hannah stepped over the bodies. "Are y-you-"

"Just keep moving."

Every time a shadow detached from the surrounding darkness, Hannah flinched. Waiting to be shot herself. Every now and then she'd hear a shot, the whine of a bullet, a flair, but so far, so good. She was still in one piece, and upright.

They moved across the deck with his men, who, seeing her with Grayson, parted like the black sea to allow them through.

A strange man, dressed as the others, in a black, head to toe, body-hugging wetsuit, helped her down a short ladder to a lower deck—probably a dive platform—where a fat, fishing boat rocked on the wavelets slapping the hull of the bigger yacht. Gray followed her onto the wood deck of the fishing boat.

Gray steadied her as the boat rocked, directing her inside a small pilothouse where a man stood, clearly ready to take off. He indicated a bench seat out of the way. Shell shocked, Hannah sat down, Gray beside her.

Taking both her hands in his, he said quietly, with an urgency she only sensed, because his eyes, his voice, his entire demeanor seemed utterly calm, "Tell me exactly what you heard."

His hands felt warm around her icy fingers. He was in control. Calm. Focused. She felt as though the only thing keeping her from screaming like a girl was Grayson's firm hold on her. "I'd just walked from the bathroom into the cabin when I heard two men talking right outside the door."

The fishing boat started pulling away from the mountainous white hull of the bigger ship. She'd never been happier to leave a place in her life. "It was something like...'Savrov used my name,'" she deepened her voice. "'Get rid of him.' The other man said, 'Permanently?' The first guy didn't say anything else for a few seconds, which I presumed meant he either gave the guy a look, or the answer was rhetorical, then he said, 'Is it set?'"

The green blinking lights near the wheel made Grayson's face look a little demonic. Still, Hannah wanted to fling herself into his arms and have him hold her tightly until her heart settled into a normal rhythm, 'til nervous sweat wasn't making her eyes burn, and the smell of dead people was a distant memory.

"He could've been referring to a date, a clock, the table."

"Funny." Hannah continued, "'As you instructed, exactly thirty minutes.' Then the other guy said, Get the chopper. I want to be out on open water to watch the show.' Which meant...there's a bomb on board."

She realized as she finished talking, that Gray's mouth was moving at the same time. She hadn't noticed in the dark, and lost momentarily in her own fear. Clearly he was talking into his unseen communications devise to his men. It was like a simultaneous translation, as he relayed everything she said to someone...somewhere while she talked. "You got the part about the bomb, right?" she echoed.

"I heard. Yo, Salina? Can this thing go any faster?" he shouted, addressing the man at the wheel. "Do you remember anything more about the conversation? Any idea who they were?"

"I recognized their voices. One served us dinner, the other was one of the bodyguards, I think."

"Was that the guy on the stairs back there?" He asked, but he didn't think so. The timing was right, but it didn't sound like the convo of two underlings.

"Hard to recognize someone without a face." She let out a short, broken breath. Her pupils were dilated, her eyes black but for small rims of vivid blue. "Why would they blow up their multimillion-dollar boat? It doesn't make sense."

"Not their boat. They hijacked it thousands of miles from here, made it their own. If they wanted to lure investors with serious bank, they had to look like they didn't need it. What was the buy in, do you know?"

"Colton took just over five million dollars."

"Jesus. The Moms had that much?"

Hannah shrugged. She'd been surprised, too. "Provenance Inc. has always done really well. They buy well, and we have a lot of steady customers from all over the country."

"You're the heart of the store, Hannah. Your creativity, and organizational skills have kept it going long after the Moms lost interest in having a shop."

Hannah's heart melted a little at the compliment, which surprised her, because she hadn't really thought she'd contributed anything but a warm body to ring up the sales. She drew in a shuddering breath as Grayson communicated with the men.

His profile, limned by the green glow, looked harsh and grim. As hard and unyielding his expression, she still would've liked to crawl into his lap and bury her face against his chest until this all magically went away.

This entire situation was surreal. Adrenaline surged through her body, and her heart beat so hard she felt it in her fingertips.

"Get the lead out, Salinas!" he yelled. "We have *maybe* ten minutes if we're lucky! By which time we need to be far, far away."

Ten freaking minutes didn't sound long enough to be far, far away, but Hannah presumed Grayson knew what he was doing. She didn't know what he was doing, but that was par for their course. "Good. Because far, far away is exactly where I want to be."

SEVEN

Before they were clear of the blast zone the fancy Megayacht blew to fucking, spectacular, hell.

Wrapping his arms around her like steel bands, Gray pressed her face against his chest, and flung them both off the bench. A percussion wave slammed against the hull of the trawler and bounced it like a toy, high on a swell.

When he needed speed, he had nothing but slow and lumbering from the old fishing boat as it bobbed and gyred on the crests.

Shockwaves from the blast surged beneath the hull. The wooden boat creaked in protest, torqueing as it pitched.

Cradling the back of her head and butt for the impact, Gray's hands took the brunt as they slammed onto the wooden floor with a jarring thud. Limbs tangled, her hair a fragrant screen over his wrist, he protected her body with his.

Hannah fought him like a wild cat. "Damn it, Gr—" She let out a muffled, blood curdling shriek directly into his ear as the sky lit up, and the boat rocked with the tumultuous waves caused by a second massive explosion.

The small boat plunged into a trough, leaving his breath at the peak of the wave for several seconds. The percussion of the explosions was enough to turn him deaf for several minutes as the blood pulsed in his ears, and his breath returned. For the first time in his ten-year career with T-FLAC, Grayson felt heart-pounding fear. Not for himself, for Hannah. He'd take another bullet, suck up the pain and trauma of being tortured in a hellhole, rather than put her in the path of...this.

Sometimes he hated his fucking job.

Tonight was one of those times.

They were impossibly far from land. . .

Grayson held most of his weight off her using his elbows, but covered as much of her as he could with his body. Grunting she tried to wiggle free. There'd been a time when this position would have her wrapping her long legs around his hips, when the hands shoving at him, would instead curl around his shoulders. When she would have reached up, pulled his head down to close the small gap between their mouths, and kissed him until neither could breathe. There'd been a time.

"Squashing-" she panted, bucking her hips, eyes a little manic in the dim light as she started to get panicky. He knew she had a tendency to claustrophobia in confined spaces, but there were no other options right now.

Easing his chest off hers by another inch, Gray stroked the hair off her sweaty forehead. "Hang on," he told her, keeping his voice calm and even, not easy bouncing around as if they were on a fun ride at the carnival. "It'll take a while to get clear. This tub wasn't built for speed."

Murmuring acceptance, she closed her eyes and lay still, but he felt the tension ripple through her body and felt the hard knocking of her heartbeat, flush against his chest. Brushing a light kiss to her temple, he murmured, "This used to be your second favorite position, remember?"

"No."

He smiled into her hair. "You'd make me flip over, then drive me insane kissing your way down my chest, your hands-" would cup his balls, and make his body arch into those small, cool, fingers as she tormented him with her soft lips, and hot avid mouth.

"To say that bringing that up, here and now, is inappropriate is an understatement, Grayson. Just shut the hell up until this is over. I can only deal with one annoyance at a freaking time."

But it got her mind off the very real danger they were in. The crashes, bangs and blunt force projectiles sounded as if they were in a war zone. Every loud noise made Hannah flinch, although he knew she tried not to by the way her body stiffened each time. Holding herself rigid under him, she was breathing hard, and her eyes were all pupil.

He combed gentle fingers through the hair at her nape. Her erogenous zone, hopefully she'd be distracted. "You'd skim your lips down my belly, remember Tink? Jesus. I was turned on by the cool strands of your hair trailing down my chest, and the anticipation of your hot, avid mouth closing around my dick." Every tactile memory was carved in his brain and indelibly imprinted in his synapses.

"Can't hear you-" A bright orange flare, another furnace blast of heat, accompanied another blast. The small boat gyrated, rising at a perilous angle up another peak. "Holy crap! How long is this going to go on?"

"Till it's over." Tightening his grip on her as the boat seemed to levitate, hang in space for a few long seconds, then with the jarring impact of a bag of cement flung from a great height, they hit a trough. The force rattled his bones as Gray buried his face beside hers to protect her from the worst of it.

ر

Even inside the small wheelhouse, protected by the walls and windows, the blast of heat on his exposed face, throat and hands was intense. He and his men were protected from the worst of it by their LockOut, but Hannah, in her jeans and thin cotton shirt was not. He was all that was between her and the incredible heat from the blast.

Projectiles from the explosion crashed onto the deck of their boat. His team, on board with them communicated through his comm as they attempted to stay clear, hang on, and put out multiple fires.

The trawler shimmied and rocked, indicating the massive size of the blast. Clearly the tangos hadn't wanted anything to remain. Whoever had set the explosives knew what they were doing. The destruction was massive, total and quick. Heavy chunks of debris struck with thuds, cracks and clangs against their boat.

The hellaciously loud crashes and thuds of shit hitting the deck and wheelhouse petered out gradually, until there was nothing more than the throb of the engines and the distant splashing as debris hit the water out of range. The rank chemical stink of burning rubber, oil, wood and ship parts made his eyes burn.

After what seemed like a lifetime, but was actually only about ten minutes, Grayson lifted his head.

"Is it over now?" Hannah shouted over the noise.

He flinched as something hard slammed into his shoulder, bracing so the impact didn't transfer to her. "We'll be out of range soon. Stay put." Not that he was giving her any choice. He wasn't budging until he had the all clear.

Through the shattered windows of the wheelhouse, he saw his men running through the smoke on deck, putting out the

fires caused by flying, flaming debris. Hannah's safety was his top priority, but so were his men. He needed to know if they'd all made it off the yacht.

His comm had fallen free, Grayson found it by feeling around near Hannah's head, then inserted it back in his ear. Her pale face was a whitish blur in the darkness, then flushed gold with each fiery flare.

Vision fuzzy, ears ringing, he checked his men. "Alpha One. Bravo, what's the ETA on our ride?"

"Bravo One. Forty-seven minutes. They'll arrive fueled and ready to go wheels up on your word. We're two clicks from hangar with our packages. One damaged." With a fifteen minute head, start Bravo team was almost there. Esmeraldas, the major seaport of northwestern Ecuador, lay on the Pacific coast. The derelict airfield they'd commandeered, was close enough to the docks for convenience, and distanced enough to make their coming and goings relatively unremarkable. The jet, fueling elsewhere, ensured a fast exit.

"Clear," Salinas spoke loudly through Gray's earpiece as he rose from his crouch beside the wheel.

Grayson bet there'd be nary a stick in the water to show the luxury ship had ever been there when it was over. Perhaps just an oil slick, but he guessed that would probably incinerate as well.

Helping Hannah to her feet, he kept a tight grip on her hand as he edged her back down onto the narrow wood seat. Sitting beside her he maintained a steadying hold, both hands bracing her shoulders as the ship rocked.

Scanning her face, Gray hoped to hell that dark shadow on her cheekbone was dirt and not a bruise. He'd always wanted to protect her because of how deceptively fragile she appeared.

But he knew she was anything but. People underestimated her grit and stubbornness because she looked ethereal. Little did they know she had steel for a backbone, and carried the troubles of her family and his on her slender shoulders. She always had.

Hannah steadily met his gaze, the blue of her eyes lost in pupil, flames from the burning ship, shooting into the night sky behind him reflected in the dark pinpoints. He didn't miss the tremble in her white-knuckled fingers, clenched in her lap.

Wrapping her hands around his wrists, when he grabbed her shoulders to steady her, her nails dug into his skin as the fishing boat continued to rock unevenly, slewing sideways.

"How can you be so calm? It's like being inside Dante's Inferno."

He braced his feet. "Having you here, puts a whole different spin on it," he said dryly, scanning her from head to toe to assure himself she wasn't hurt.

Running his thumbs over her collarbone as he held her, he felt the rapid-fire beat of her pulse in her neck. She closed her eyes for a moment as he held onto her. His own heart beat triple time. If he hadn't moved fast enough to get her off the ship, if anything had happened...Gray's blood chilled. She shouldn't be here. Shouldn't be any-fucking-where near here. His brother had a lot to answer for. A lot.

As much as he'd like to forget the shitstorm going on around them, when he deemed the explosive part of the fireworks over, Gray eventually dropped his hands, instantly missing the touch of her fingers on his wrists.

"Okay?"

She nodded, her tangled hair covering her cheek. Shoving it aside with fingers that still trembled, she lifted her chin. "I'd rather be sitting in the back row of the movie theatre eating popcorn, than inside this live action, I can tell you that! You really are Jason Bourne."

"Nothing as glamorous." He stroked his thumb lightly over the smudge on her cheek. Dirt, thank God. "Black ops. No one was supposed to know."

"Even your fiancé?" Her tone was even, but pain flashed in her eyes. "If we'd married, would you have kept disappearing, not telling me where you were, or if you were alive? Would I ever have known if you'd died protecting the world?"

"I would've told you—eventually."

"We wouldn't know if you were dead or alive. How can you live with doing that to the people who love you? I hate secrets. They're bad for the one in the dark, and bad for the one holding them. People who keep secrets tend to be depressed, stressed and isolated. Any of that sound familiar?"

"Don't shrink me. Let's put this conversation off for now." He glanced over at Salinas to see if he was taking it all in.

Didn't appear to be.

"That means never. Got it," she said tightly, following his gaze. "Back to work?"

"In a minute..." He touched the rapid pulse at the base of her throat because he couldn't—not. A few more minutes weren't going to change the course of history. Her skin, cool, a little clammy with nerves, was still as soft as the petal of a rose. He wanted to inhale her and drench himself in her sweetness.

She went through a series of hacking coughs. All he could do was stroke her back until it subsided, then wipe the tears off her cheeks with both thumbs.

She gave him a helpless, frustrated look, then pushed his hands away. "Don't baby me. I'm scared, confused, and will probably burst into tears at any second. Give me a second to get my spine back."

He kept his hands to himself with sheer willpower. "Nah. My Tink has a spine of steel."

She sighed. "If only."

The smell of the days catch was still present, though mostly masked by the strong stench of burning wood, fiberglass, and oil. Thick black smoke hung low over the dark water, drifting to them on the wind, making their eyes water, and catching roughly in their throats. The oily fumes clogged his throat, and made Hannah cough again.

"Targets secure?" Eyes on her, he spoke into the comm. Using the comm was more effective than waiting for everyone's hearing to return to normal. The sea settled down as the trawler distanced itself from the scene. Lessening the blast of heat, their movement carried them away from the worst of the smoke and debris.

"Yeah. Two boats headed in. We had a few casualties," LeRoy Salinas, piloting the boat, used his comm, despite standing less than ten feet away. "Nothing anyone cried about," his voice was dry.

EIGHT

W hich boat has my brother?"

"He was with Alverez on the first one in," one of his men out on deck responded. "Saw them on deck just before we left."

Good. Gray wasn't done with his brother—not by a long shot.

Hannah turned on the bench seat to look at the flames shooting up into the blackness of the sky and reflecting orange off the low hanging clouds. "My God." She shuddered. "It's a miracle we got away in time."

Pulling her back against his chest, he wrapped his arms around her waist, curving his fingers into the belt loop of her jeans. She resisted for a moment, then let out a frustrated breath and leaned her head into his shoulder. Together they watched the flames in the distance. A bonfire against the blackness of the night sky, reflected dancing flames in the inky water.

Resting his chin on her hair, Gray listened as his men checked in. "Any chatter on Stonefish?" he asked, feeling the slump of Hannah's body relaxing into him as the adrenaline leaked out of her, leaving her limp and exhausted.

"Nada."

"Bravo One." Charlie Kyatta ID'ed himself briskly. "At location. Mauro's gut shot. Jaramillo says he's not going to make it. We have Sorenson and Deeks separated, but so far neither are talkin'."

Charlie Kyatta and Bravo team weren't wasting a second trying to pull any intel that would help them in the next phase. Finding Stonefish and stopping him before he set into motion a coup no one would be able to stop.

"Inform Deeks we have his sister and niece," Grayson, voice cold, reminded the team leader. "Tell Sorenson we'll withhold all meds until he gives us what we want." Sorenson had had a heart transplant barely three months earlier. Acute cellular rejection was most common in patients the first three to six months after a transplant. This was nasty business, but they were prepared to do whatever it took. The countdown was going fast. They had to find Stonefish before it was too fucking late.

"Are you done with work for just a minute?" Hannah asked, turning in his arms. Her husky voice ruffled primeval nerve endings, he'd kept tamped for years.

He had to smile, because just looking at her lightened his heart. "Yeah." For about eight minutes until they reached the dock.

"You know I hate you, right?" she whispered, voice clogged with emotion. It was dim in the wheelhouse. Just the ambient glow of the rapidly retreating fire, and the small lights on the dash across the room. Hair disheveled, white shirt covered with dark, smoky blotches, she was a red-hot mess. Which made her, blotches, smudges and all, just about the sexiest thing he'd ever seen. He'd never get tired of looking at her.

Grayson's smile disappeared, as his heart pinched. Yeah. He knew how she felt about him. With just cause, but it didn't fucking break his heart any less.

He turned off his comm. His men knew what had to be done, and he had less minutes to hold Hannah before he put her on a plane back to Chicago. There was no guarantee he'd ever see her again. "Hannah-"

"Don't think I'm downplaying how I feel. The love I once felt for you, a love that was unconditional, and forever, morphed into a feeling that makes me heartsick. I want to not feel this way. But I can't make myself – *not*. You ripped out my heart without a word." She leaned forward, spreading her palms on his chest.

"You killed something inside me, and I resent that just as much. I miss who I was with you. I want that woman back, Grayson. But she's gone. My anger and hurt built up and built up with nowhere to go. I didn't expect to ever see you again. I sure as hell didn't expect it to be here. Now." Her throat moved as she swallowed, her reddened eyes, holding his, were dark and liquid with emotion. "I'd barely recovered. I don't want to see you and rehash, re-feel that ever again."

"We have a second chance."

Putting cool fingers over his lips she shook her head. "Too late for second chances. But physically I still want what my brain tells me is bad for me. So I want you to kiss me, Gray. So I know my memory is playing tricks on me, so that I know that nothing could be that electrifying, that magical. Kiss me like you kissed me on my seventeenth birthday. As if you'd die if you didn't..."

He'd kissed her earlier, but he sensed she was looking for some sort of closure. He'd die if he didn't give her what she was asking for, and change her mind, right now. He felt a familiar stirring as he wrapped his arms around her, tugging her softness close.

He wanted to strip her naked, and take her right there on the bench. Jesus. He'd lost his fucking mind. Since when did he allow himself to experience any emotions? Or think about anything other than the op? He made do with limiting himself to caressing her back through her shirt. He traced the rapid pulse at the base her throat with gentle lips. She smelled of smoke and flowers, and he tasted the sweat on her still damp skin. His dick, constrained behind the equivalent of a sports cup, leapt in anticipation as he bit her earlobe and reveled in her full body shudder.

Hannah splayed her palms on his chest, kneading her fingers like a cat, as he gently scored the tendons of her neck with his teeth, then stroked his lips up, over her jaw to her mouth.

"This is just to purge those memories," her breath snagged as he stroked his tongue around her ear lobe. "You get that, right?"

"After this it'll be just a distant memory," he assured her, loving her shudder as he breathed against the damp trail he'd made up the side of her throat. He was going to make sure they made new ones.

"Good."

"Perfect." Tempting as it was to linger, take his time, draw out the anticipation- It had been way too fucking long. That kiss earlier had been merely an appetizer. This couldn't be a full meal either, there were far too many eyes around, and interruption was inevitable.

Gray wanted her tongue in his mouth. Now. Her breath hitched as he parted her lips with a languid sweep of his tongue. Slick. Hot. Eager.

He took his time, savoring instead of devouring, letting his tongue slide along hers. Teasing. Tasting. Sucking.

Hannah boldly matched him stroke for stroke, until they were both breathing harshly. Through the thin cotton of her shirt he felt her heat as he used his palm in the small of her back to hold her tightly against him.

She blew his mind. Rocked his world. Always had. Always would.

"ETA ten minutes," Salinas said discreetly in his ear, through the comm, bringing Grayson back to reality with a thud.

Reluctantly he withdrew his mouth from Hannah's. Her eyes were dark, her mouth damp. His groin ached, and his heart felt buoyant. Holding her gaze, he responded. "Copy that."

Breathing rough, color high, she leaned away from him, scanning his face. "It's dizzying how quickly you can turn on and off like that. It's your Super Power, isn't it? The ability to disengage and turn off your emotions?"

"It's the first time my work and personal life have collided. There's a reason most T-FLAC operatives have no personal lives. This job is all consuming. But it killed me that you believed- Jesus, Hannah, I hoped you knew me." It killed him that she'd believed the worst of him, despite knowing each other for most of their lives.

Hannah turned her head to look at him, her hair snagging in his bristly unshaven jaw. "I thought I knew you, too. But boy, was I wrong. I don't know which man scares me more," she said quietly. "The Grayson I believed for years was a criminal, or the man I just saw kill several men without hesitation while saying he's the good guy."

Jesus that stung. "You know I'd never hurt you, right?"

Hannah lifted an eloquent brow. "You think it was painless being left at the altar?"

Ouch.

He sucked in a breath of her honey and orange blossom shampoo, almost overpowered by the stink of smoke. The good and the ugly. The juxtaposition wasn't lost on him. "Mitigating circumstances," he said roughly. This was neither the time nor place to tell her the why of it. Maybe he'd never have that chance, but he sure as shit wasn't going to waste this moment rehashing what had happened to prevent his returning home to her on time.

"Maybe sometime I'll give enough of a damn to ask what they were." Her hard ass words were ruined by the catch in her voice.

Ah, Hannah. "I do my job. And I'm good at it. No apologies. What my men and I do matters. It keeps people safe when they aren't even aware of being in danger. They don't have to know the who and why of it."

She was quiet for several minutes. "That bomb would've gone off with us on board. We're lucky you showed up."

Grayson's smile felt strained. He saw the lights of the city in the distance. Time was almost up. "Colton isn't going to feel so damned grateful when I strip his skin from his bones."

"I'll help you." Hannah assured him, then shifted out of his arms, leaving Gray feeling bereft, and cold. She'd always been instinctively tuned into other people's needs—frequently to the detriment of her own. Had she kissed him because she knew how desperately he needed her? Or was the need her own, as she'd said? Gray used to be able to read her, but not anymore. She'd become adept at masking her innermost feelings.

And no doubt he could take credit for that. It was as if he'd told her he didn't believe in fairies, and her light had died.

Sliding back across the wood bench, she clasped her fingers in her lap, and gave him a steady, unemotional look. They could be strangers. "I imagine you don't want these men to see you all over me. Go. Do whatever it is you have to do. I'm fine in here."

Gray wavered between duty and desire. There was no fucking time to talk it out. No time to mend what he'd broken. He knew where he needed to be, but was also acutely aware of where he wanted to be. Here in this temporary bubble with Hannah. Holding her had been too good to be true. Her long-lashed, big blue eyes looked bruised, and wary. Gray pushed to his feet. He was a fool to think he had a choice. There was none. In less than thirty hours, Stonefish would reign terror on South America. He had to be apprehended and stopped.

"We'll be docking at Esmeraldas in a few minutes," he told her, voice brisk as he got to his feet. "You'll be on your way home in less than an hour."

"What about Colton? What about the Moms' money which is the whole frigging reason I'm here in the first place?"

"I have no fucking idea, Hannah," Frustration, rage, shame, and lust tangled in his gut. "I'll try and help you sort it out when I've done what I came here for." Stonefish needed those diamonds to pay for the weapons he'd ordered. No diamonds, no weapons.

No money for Hannah to take home.

But the principals must have the diamonds *somewhere*. They wouldn't have blown the ship without ensuring the stones went with them when they bailed.

"You know what, Grayson? Go ahead and do your job. And I'll take care of Colton and the Moms problems as I've always done."

A car awaited them at the docks. Grayson didn't bother with the niceties of introducing her to his team. They got in the car, and drove through Esmeraldas, which had rolled up its streets hours ago.

Kissing him had been a colossal mistake. Hannah knew it before she instigated it. But having shit blow up, men running around shooting at each other, blood and death everywhere, Colton in it up to his eyeballs and Grayson in the mix, made her realize something. If she was going out with a bang, she wanted to be with Grayson when it happened. Even now, she knew she'd kiss him again given half the chance. God. She was screwed up. Hot then cold. She couldn't get home soon enough, and out of Grayson's force field.

Really, at home she- if not hated his guts- felt profoundly. . . negative emotions. Yet the second she saw him after three years, her emotions went haywire and she all but begged him to ravish her. Ravish was a good word.

Not that there'd be any ravishing in her future. She sighed.

"Hannah? I asked if you're okay?"

She turned to face him. "Don't ask me questions you don't want an honest answer to," she whispered, a snap in her voice she couldn't help. Cranky and annoyed, she hoped the others with them were completely deaf, as well as oblivious to the thick undercurrent in the car as they bounced over a scrub grass field.

There was no light, not even headlights. The man who'd piloted the fishing boat, and was now driving, had pulled down what she presumed were night vision glasses as soon as they'd reached the edge of town. She of course, saw nothing but black.

Just like her relationship with Grayson Burke.

"Why don't you guys just drop me at the main terminal, and I'll see myself home?" Not that she saw a terminal anywhere near where they were. But there must be one. It was an airport.

Gray's eyes glittered in the dim lighting inside the vehicle as they pulled up to the dark hulk of a large building. "No money. No passport."

Hannah refrained from saying, "Fuck you."

Barely.

NINE

When they got out of the vehicle, the interior lights didn't go on. Hannah stepped out after Gray. Dry grass crunched under her feet. Almost pitch dark, cool, and absolutely still, there wasn't a breath of wind. A shiver of foreboding raced up her back, damp with nervous perspiration. "Is this why they call it black ops?" she asked facetiously, keeping her voice down because it was freakishly quiet.

She really, really, really wanted to be home, watching TV in her jammies, eating her Friday night tablespoon of Ben & Jerry's Chocolate Fudge Brownie. She wanted to forget what Colton had dragged her into. She wanted him safely back at the insurance company where he worked. Wanted to re-forget Grayson. She wanted the Moms home from Asia so she could quit managing Provenance Inc.

She also wanted *not* to feel like crap, because having hypoglycemic issues really wasn't convenient right now.

That was a long list of freaking wants. But that's about as far as Hannah got. Because she couldn't think further than getting through this ordeal right now.

The hangar was about a hundred feet away, an enormous, black square against the night sky. Silently she trudged along between Grayson and a man built like a tank. Two of his men walked in front of her, a male and a female operative behind. All dressed in black, so they pretty much blended into the darkness.

"Do you think I'll try and make a break for it? Run across a dark field in a strange town with no money and no identification?" she asked with just a touch of sarcasm.

"Keep your voice down," he said so quietly she shouldn't have been able to hear him, yet even as soft as his voice was, she heard every word. "We don't know if Stonefish has more of his people around. We're not taking any chances."

Fabulous. Now she felt as though she had a bullseye in the middle of her back. This morning she hadn't known any spies other than Bourne and Bond. Now she was surrounded by the real deal. It seemed a lifetime ago, instead of hours earlier, that she and Colton had boarded the *Stone's Throw*, and since then her life had taken a weird, scary turn.

Being surrounded by Gray's men was like walking inside the high walls of a black cave. Hannah was relieved when they entered the hangar through a side door. Blinking in the brilliant overhead lights flooding the vast empty space, she wasn't sorry when the men peeled off. Grayson, however, stayed glued to her side.

She shot him a glance. Focused and fierce, he strode into the center of the large space, keeping her within reach of his hand even though he didn't touch her. She always forgot how tall he was until he was standing right next to her. Six three, of disreputable male, with his darkly stubbled jaw, dark, dangerous glower, and the skintight black outfit that displayed his tall, virile physique to perfection. He looked tough, mean and dangerous as hell. "I wouldn't want to bump into you in a dark alley," she told him sotto voce, as she sped up to match his long strides.

It was disconcerting to realize that she didn't know this Grayson at all.

"Trust me," he said, scanning the open space and milling people as if looking for ninjas to jump out from every corner. Which, God only knew, wouldn't surprise Hannah in the least. "You'd want me with you in that dark alley."

She rubbed the faint, annoying headache at her temples with two fingers. "Fortunately, I don't frequent that many dark alleys."

He slanted her a look, gray eyes softening. "I know you're freaked out by all this, but hang tough, Tink. Stay with me until we can establish who's who, okay?"

Now that the danger was past, Hannah realized she wasn't feeling so hot. Nerves, stress, a bouncing boat. Low blood sugar. Shit. She shrugged. "I have nothing better to do."

The hangar was old, and probably not in use. Rusted, corrugated walls, oil-stained cement floor, and a bunch of broken packing crates piled haphazardly in the far corner. Half the overhead lights were burned out or hanging by electrical wires.

Thirsty, she tuned out the susurrus of multiple conversations, looking around for something to drink.

A soda would help with her blood sugar until she could get some real food. There didn't appear to be a vending machine around. But considering the look of the hangar, if there were, anything in it would be petrified by now.

Other than swarming people, and mounds of windswept leaves and debris in the corners, the space was empty. Just a few large grease spots where planes once sat. Grayson's men, dressed in identical sleek black get-ups, cowls shoved back, were starting to separate the swarms of people from the ship.

The process was loud, and she learned a few new swear words, as everyone voiced their opinions more loudly than the guy next to him. It was a big crowd of crazy.

"The plane will be here soon," Grayson told her, giving her a small portion of his attention.

She stepped back. "I'll stay out of your way."

He locked his hand around her wrist. "No, stick to me like white on rice. I don't want you out of my sight."

Tempted to remind him that he wasn't the boss of her in any way, shape or form, Hannah bit her tongue and tugged herself out of his hold. The reality was he was the only man here that she trusted; she just didn't trust him to touch her.

Seeing a familiar gleaming, sandy blond head among the crowd, she indicated his brother with a jerk of her chin. "Colton's over there. God. He looks terrified."

"Good," Gray said unsympathetically. "I don't want you near him until he's been processed."

"Come on, Grayson. You know he wasn't aware of who he was dealing with."

"No one with half a fucking brain goes into business without knowing everything there is to know about his partners. But let me rephrase that. Would he steal multimillions of dollars from his mother? No. He's too fucking good for that."

Hannah had never heard the suppressed brutality in his voice before, as he said what she'd been thinking. "Would he take you on board a ship half a world away to fucking impress you, but in fact, plop you into the lap of not just a terrorist, but a *group* of terrorists whose leader is number one on half a dozen countries' fucking watch lists!"

"Stop Gray. He didn't know they were terrorists." Man, she was so not up to sparring with Grayson right now. She needed all her cylinders firing at full throttle to keep up with him as it was.

No way to measure her blood sugar since everything she owned was at the bottom of the South Pacific. But if her blurry vision and other symptoms were any indication, it was low.

"He's a *criminal*, Hannah. He stole the Moms' life savings, and more. The buy in for investors was ten mil a piece- What? You weren't aware of the full amount?"

"You must be mistaken. Provenance Inc. is doing well, really well, but they didn't have that kind of money. I estimated he took somewhere in the region of five million."

"Well then he stole the rest from someone else." Grayson said grimly. "We'll know after he's been questioned. Make no mistake, he*will* be prosecuted, and there's a damn good chance he'll spend some formative years behind bars. If nothing else, this should put the fear of God into him, and teach him not to fucking steal, especially from his own family."

"That horse bolted out of the stable a long time ago," Hannah said dryly, really wanting to sit down now. Colton had to be punished, but she just wanted to get through the next few hours before she had the reality check that her friend not only deserved to go to jail, but that she'd be the one pressing charges.

Gray stopped to talk to a short, muscular, redhead She recognized most of the men she'd seen on board *Stone's Throw*. Two of the three men who'd given the impressive presentation about the hotel complex, Elijah Sorenson and William Deeks were each being questioned by several black-clad T-FLAC men, fifty feet apart. They both had their hands cuffed behind their backs, and some sort of hobble around their ankles. By their identical expressions, they were clearly pissed off and uncooperative.

A dozen crewmembers, dressed in shorts and white shirts with *Stone's Throw* insignias on the breast pocket, were similarly hobbled. They all looked unhappy and scared as they were individually questioned in various parts of the hangar.

Hannah shivered, rubbing her upper arms briskly against the chill. She wanted Gray's arms around her. Or a big fluffy blanket. No blanket in sight, and of course he didn't touch her. Maybe it was better he didn't.

"Copy that. Tell him he's on his own in this clusterfuck. Kyatta and Bren Edde to me. Out." he said with ill suppressed anger to whoever was talking to him in his earpiece. "Colton's asking for you," he told her, the anger still a dark thread in his voice.

"I have absolutely no desire to see him. Ever, as a matter of fact. That's probably going to mess up Thanksgiving dinners," she added dryly as he continued walking, expecting her to catch up, "but I'll live with that." She had to practically jog to keep up with Gray's long strides.

Hannah knew at any minute another of his men would need him for something, and he'd forget she was there. "What are you going to do with all these people?"

"Question them here, then transport them to Montana."

"Montana?"

"T-FLAC Headquarters."

She pretty much knew they wouldn't be taking a detour to Chicago to drop her off. She didn't feel so hot. All she wanted was to get as far away from what was going on, eat, and sleep.

She needed to eat. Soon. The adrenaline had worn off, and she was feeling shaky and weak.

Gray stopped in his tracks, turned and searched her face, then frowned as he cupped her cheek. "You're cold and clammy."

She tilted her head a little so her cheek rested in his warm palm, like a sleepy kitten. "That sounded like an accusation."

"Fuck. You gave yourself a shot just before I found you, and you haven't eaten. Your blood sugar's dropping, isn't it?"

She'd timed her shot just before dinner. But dinner had never happened. She didn't have any way to test her blood glucose level, but she knew it was way too low. She should've eaten hours ago.

As much as she wanted to rest her face in his palm like a pet for a few hours, Hannah stepped out of reach. "We've been a little busy. But getting something to eat soon would be good."

"Anyone got any hard candy?" he said into his comm, which earned him a few surprised glances from the operatives. "We've got a diabetic here. She needs something. Search everyone again. Candy. Gum. Anything."

"Thanks," she said quietly.

"How bad do you feel?"

"Get me that candy," she said calmly, rubbing the headache at her temple with fingers that shook.

He touched the comm as Kyatta and Bren Edde strode toward him. "Find me that fucking candy, people!"

TEN

hile we're waiting, let's find the people you overheard, and see who this Savrov insulted by using his name," Gray told her. He touched his ear. "Bring me a guy called Savrov."

"They were going to kill him, maybe he's dead," Hannah reminded him.

"Maybe, but I don't think there was enough time between when you overhead them and when I found you. I believe the men you overheard were the two I saw in the corridor."

"Get the lead out, people! Where the fuck is Savrov?" Gray said into his communications devise.

It took several minutes, but there was, apparently, no Savrov in the hangar. Everyone was accounted for.

Feeling a little light-headed, Hannah rubbed her upper arms, not sure if she was hot or cold. "He could've been one of the people that were left dead on the ship."

"Strong possibility on that. Hang on a sec. I don't see Mauro, did he make it?" Grayson asked tightly into the comm, then listened to the response. Easier than yelling across the enormous space, Hannah knew, but she would've liked to know more than just half the conversation. And even that was in some form of verbal shorthand.

"Shit," he snarled, after listening to something transmitted into his earpiece.

A dead end, Hannah thought with black humor. Until today, she'd never seen a dead body, now she was getting frighteningly used to seeing a lot of them.

"Considering the timing, I think the man on the stairs was one of the men you overheard," Gray turned his attention back to her. Under normal circumstances it would be difficult to keep track of who he was talking to, but right now, Hannah was having difficulty navigating her way around a normal conversation. Her mental focus and her vision were both getting fuzzy.

"The other guy's a crewmember. He's here. None of them were KIA."

Trying to corral her wandering thoughts, she gave him a blank look.

"Killed in action. I shot a bodyguard on the stairs, he could be our boss man. He was with a crewman, who'll be able to ID him, for us." He wrapped his hand around her upper arm and steadied her. Hannah didn't even realize she'd been swaying slightly. "Would you recognize the man's voice if you heard it again?"

Frowning hurt her head. "Who? The dead guy?" Hannah impatiently rubbed the annoying headache pulsing at her temples. "Of course." God she was cranky and confused. The nervousness, and desire to pick a fight could be attributed to the circumstances, but she knew her body, and was familiar with the symptoms. Cold and clammy, she was freaking *starving*, and her heart pounded with anxiety. Hypoglycemia, probably exacerbated by her present circumstances.

"How long until the plane gets here?" If it was big enough to make the long flight, and there were dozens of people expected on board, there'd be food. Something to drink.

He glanced over her shoulder. "It arrived a few minutes ago. Thanks," he said to a woman dressed as he was, as she handed him a can of Coke. He gave it to Hannah.

She frowned at it. "Where did this materialize from?"

"Hensley went to get it from the plane. Here," he said gently, taking the can back. "Let me open that for you."

She was pretty sure she could open her own damned drink, but right now she couldn't quite figure out how.

He wrapped his large, warm hand around hers, lifted it to her mouth. "Drink."

Opening her mouth, Hannah let the fizzy, overly sweet soda slide down her throat. He tangled the fingers of his other hand in her hair, holding the back of her head to assist her. She needed all the help she could get. Her brain was going in slo-mo.

"Drink it all, honey, the sugar will help you feel better."

She did so, her fingers curled around his wrist as she drank. She couldn't fight low blood sugar and Grayson at the same time. Hells-bells, she could barely keep one thought in her head at a time at the moment.

"You scare the shit out of me, you know that, Tink? Not your fault. But fuckit, you need a keeper."

"I really don't," she said tartly, moving away so his hand dropped. Drinking the soda helped. A lot. And she felt more lucid by the minute as the sugar hit her system. "I was only supposed to be here a couple of days at the most. I came prepared with enough insulin for two *weeks*, and a whole bag of snacks and candy for emergencies. I didn't know I was going to be kidnapped and forced to leave all my belongings on a doomed ship."

He brushed her cheek, gray eyes searching her face. "There's that."

Self-conscious, she combed her fingers through the tangled stands of her hair. Her makeup must have sweated off hours ago, and she probably had raccoon eyes.

Putting her palm on the hard wall of his chest, she gave a pathetically light shove, feeling the tingle of contact all the way up her arm. "You're in my personal space, and all your spylettes are watching us."

"Are you up to IDing the guy?"

He spoke into his communications device, as he watched her. His eyes made a whole slew of promises of their own. "Bring Deeks to me." He turned back to her, his eyes focused intently on hers. "What do you want him to say?"

She thought about the conversation she'd overhead. "'As you instructed. Exactly thirty minutes from now.'" Which, as it happened, had turned out to be a lot less.

"You'll recognize the voice just from that?"

"Perfect pitch, remember?"

"There isn't a damn thing about you I've forgotten." Unflinching, he held her gaze.

"Then it must be that your sense of direction is out of whack. One would think a guy like you, leading a tough-ass team like this, could find his way home. But then...one would be wrong."

"Don't doubt that I'd find you blindfolded, in the dark, on another planet," Gray murmured, voice tight.

She rolled her eyes. "Yeah, I guess finding me in my own condo was just too damn easy. Next time I'll remember to blindfold the groom and have the chapel on a sunless frigging planet."

Gray shifted his jaw. "I can tell you're feeling better." His voice was bone dry.

"Getting there."

A tall, grim-looking man, with salt and pepper hair and a craggy face, came up to Grayson. "Everyone's ready, and Deeks is hobbling his ass over here"

"Good," Hannah said, grateful for the interruption. "Let's get this over with so I can go home."

"This isn't over, Tink."

"You're a promise and three years too late, Grayson." Hannah said tartly. "Just have him say the lines so I can get the hell out of here."

#

Perfect pitch had fuck-all to do with recognizing a voice. Especially when Hannah had been afraid for her life at the time. But she was all he had right now. "Bring over Deeks."

The three terrified and loudly protesting 'investors', his baby brother included, were demanding their rights. As if they fucking had rights in a foreign country consorting with terrorists on the watch list for fucksake.

"Keep 'em on ice," Gray instructed the teams.

"What do you want to do with the crew? Take them with us, dispose of them or leave them here?" Kyatta asked in his ear as he prodded an unhealthy looking guy, with too much body fat, and a small, bald head to the lineup with the rest of the bodyguards, taking baby steps because of his ankle ties. While Gray had ordered them kept alive, their quality of life wasn't a consideration. Many of the bad guys sported bloody lips, assorted gashes, and an array of colorful bruises. A crying shame.

The crewmembers hadn't been interrogated yet. They'd know little to nothing other than they'd been minding their own business off the coast of South Africa, been hijacked, kidnapped, and forced to stay on board for the long trip to South America. They didn't know any of the people on board, other than each other, and this was the first time they'd been ashore in months. It was clear by their body language that they didn't even like one another, and wanted to get the hell away ASAP. They were lowest priority, and would be processed last.

"Yeah," Gray told Charlie. "We'll get the crew back home. Wherever that is. Keep them secured for now."

"Hang tight," he told Hannah off comm. She looked remarkably better since drinking the Coke. Her color was back, and the shaking had stopped. She'd scared the bejesus out of him when they'd gotten into the hangar and he'd seen how weak and vague she was.

Lifting her chin, Hannah gave him a cool look. "Don't you have terrorists to terrorize?"

"I have a few minutes to spare and competent people to do the terrorizing."

She rolled her eyes. "Please, don't waste your spare few minutes on me. Go to your spy stuff. I'm a big girl. I can stay out of your way and. . . observe your manly prowess."

He smiled. "You're cranky."

"Ya think?" She gave him an annoyed look. "Run along and do your spy stuff, so I can get over it."

The aftermath of a blast of adrenaline affected most people that way- cranky was mild. He'd seen people go into manic rages, and go ape-shit after going through half of what

Hannah had just experienced. In her case he suspected her irritability had a lot to do with low blood sugar as well.

Thank God the plane had arrived, because Gray was pretty sure if her hypoglycemia had gotten worse, she'd be in a fucking *coma,* and not giving him sass, right now. The knowledge that he should've taken into account her illness made him sick to his stomach. And so fucking *furious* at his brother, that he wanted to pummel Colton into the ground. Twice. Once for himself. Once for her.

Shifting so he could keep an eye on Hannah, he filled his team leaders in on what she'd overheard in the corridor earlier.

Around them people were moved and realigned to form a line. "Not the crew. Not if her interpretation of the convo's correct. One of the men was clearly in charge. I killed one guy in the corridor outside the cabin she was in. Bodyguard type. Armed. He was with a crewmember. Not sure if they were the ones she overheard or not. A crewmember wouldn't have been entrusted to blow up the ship, or to make sure the diamonds were secure. So the man who gave the order must've been one of the three known principals on board. The other, a high-up associate. He glanced across at the lineup. "Anyone missing?"

"Just Mauro, remember?"

"Yeah. Double fuck." Sorenson or Deeks better give up Stonefish, otherwise this fucking mission was a bust. And they still hadn't found the diamonds. Gray hoped they were at the bottom of the ocean.

"Can you hang on a few more minutes to listen to some of these guys before you go?"

"Sure."

"One at a time, starting with you." Gray motioned to William Deeks, a forty-two year old Kenyan, dressed in a scuffed and smudged thousand dollar dark suit, open necked white shirt, and three thousand dollar shoes. The man had who'd been with Stonefish for more than twenty-two years. No known address. Sister; single-mother, small daughter. Both residing in Nairobi. The man's mahogany skin shone in overhead lights. He didn't look nervous or even fucking concerned.

"You won't make it out of Esmeraldas alive," Deeks said in a well-modulated voice, Africa tinged with British prep school as he was urgently shoved forward by Bren Edde, "let alone out of Ecuador. Stonefish is aware of T-FLAC's actions, and reprisals will be severe and swift."

"We have Adimu and Dafina," Gray responded, not missing a beat. "Where do we find your boss, and which of you has the diamonds?"

Hearing his sister and niece's names made the Kenyan jerk in response. He reined himself in pretty fast, giving Gray an inscrutable look. "You would not harm a woman and a small child." "To get my hands on Stonefish? Fuck yes, I most certainly would. Answer the question."

"No one knows where he is. We never know. As for the diamonds, the answer is clear. At the bottom of the South Pacific." "Is that your final answer?"

"It's the truth."

Not even fucking close. But there was time and the appropriate location to interrogate him elsewhere. Right now he wanted Hannah to recognize the voice, so she could leave. "Repeat this phrase. 'As you instructed. Exactly thirty minutes from now.'"

Deeks repeated the words. Hannah shook her head, and the man was returned to his corner of the hangar.

"Let's have Sorenson."

Sorenson, a white-haired man in his late fifties, sporting a tan and a soul-patch, gave him a dead-eyed-snake look. Like Deeks he wore a tailored suit and expensive shoes. He was a filthy mess, with a long rip in his pant leg, and the side of his face caked with dried blood from the nasty gash over his eye,. His tie had been removed by Gray's people. But he looked like the kind of guy who'd have the top button of his shirt done up, and a Winsor knot in some expensive neckwear.

Grayson repeated the request about Stonefish and the diamonds, threatened the man with the withholding of his medication, and was met with calm.

"Answer the damn question." Gray said coldly when the man just stood there.

"Did you miss the ship exploding?"

"Since your people initialized the blast, dickhead, we know someone ensured the rocks were safe before she blew. Isn't it time for your medication?"

"I don't know what happened to the diamonds. If I die, you will have nothing."

"If you live I have nothing." Gray said. "So what do I have to lose by letting your heart fail as I watch?" Well-trained, and loyal to a fault, Sorenson remained mute.

"Say this-"

"Fuck yo-" Suddenly the older man clutched his chest and dropped to his knees. Eyes white and wild, he gasped, "Medication."

"Sure. Repeat this first. 'As you instructed. Exactly thirty minutes from now.'"

78

Sorensen keeled over, gasping for breath, his face a rictus of pain.

"Fuck me." Gray crouched beside him to feel the pulse at his throat. Felt fine to him, but what did he know about heart transplants? "Anything you'd like to say to atone for your sins before you croak?"

"Grayson!" Hannah sounded horrified.

"Help. Me."

"Help me first, dickwad. Where's Stonefish?"

"Sir?" A crewman, close enough to witness what was happening, raised his voice to get their attention. Fortyish, bald, British. Like most of the other captives, his clothes were speckled with dried blood splatter, grease marks and smudges from the oily smoke during the explosion. A red mark that looked like a burn cut across his left cheek.

"If I may?" he said deferentially. "I, too have a heart complaint. I have medication. If I may have that returned-?" He glanced over at Kyatta.

Hannah grabbed his hand. "That's-"

"Just a minute, honey." Charlie looked at him for action. Grayson nodded. "Sure. Bring it over." It would either work, or it wouldn't. At another nod from Gray, Charlie Kyatta stooped to give Sorenson the medication.

"That's him!" Hannah grabbed his forearm with both hands. "That's the man!"

Gray observed Charlie trying to get Sorenson to open his mouth to take the damned pill. Well hell, now the guy couldn't die. "It was Sorenson?" No surprise. Sorenson was Stonefish's number one lieutenant. Sprawled on the floor, he looked like he was recovering just fine from his 'heart attack' as he aggressively forced Charlie Kyatta's hand away from his mouth.

"No. For God's sake, Grayson! Not him! The guy over there who offered to help! The crewman! He's putting on a fake English accent, but he's American. *He's* the man I heard outside the cabin."

ELEVEN

The bald guy on my nine is Stonefish," he said into his communications thingy.

Since this was the very man Grayson was trying to find, she was shocked at how cool, and emotionless, his voice was. Until she caught a glimpse of his eyes. Then the hair stood up on the back of her neck.

She had no idea how Gray had made the leap. But he had. She swiveled her attention to Stonefish, seeing in the bald guy's face the realization that he'd just been identified at the same time Gray did. Gun raised, he shifted slightly in front of her, blocking Hannah's view. "Get Hannah the fuck out of here. *Now!* Go. Go. Go."

The bald guy grabbed Colton, pressed a small knife to his throat. Tilting her friend off balance tight against him, he backed away. "Stay back! Stay back! I'll kill him!"

Colton's face drained of color, as he staggered backwards, the man's arm around his throat, the knife poised dangerously over his jugular.

Terrified for Colton's safety, Hannah turned back to Gray. His gun was raised, but he didn't shoot.

"Hold your fire," he said, barely above a whisper. "We need him alive. Hensley? Where the f-"

Ponytail bouncing, the female operative who'd brought Hannah the soda, raced over, grabbed her arm, and propelled her back toward the door at a run. "Hop to it, Girlfriend," Hensley yelled, gun in hand. "The shit's about to hit the fan."

Hannah didn't argue. She ran.

They burst through the door into a night filled with lights and more running, black-clad people. A small, white jet gleamed in the floods, and nearby a large helicopter's rotors spun slowly with an ear throbbing whop, whop, whop. Behind them, from the hangar she heard the chatter of gunfire, screams, shouts and raised voices.

The fear of being so close to this much danger was somewhat overshadowed by her fear for Colton and Gray. No matter how many times they'd had their problems, they were also two of the closest people in her life. She knew she had to get to safety, but still feared for their lives.

"This her?" A man yelled, pulling Hannah back to her surroundings. He grabbed her arm from Hensley in a grip that almost dislocated her shoulder.

"Grayson says not to let her get any holes in her! Copy?"

The man, dressed in black pants and t-shirt, touched his ear. "He's giving me instructions as we speak," he told Hensley dryly. "I've got her. Go do your thing."

Hensley gave a mock salute. "Hang with Blinston. He's one of the good guys. Nice meeting you, Girlfriend."

The man had a firm, implacable hold on her upper arm. "This way."

Hannah flinched as the pop, pop, pop of gunfire sounded closer than inside the hangar. She tried to pause, to turn, hoping to catch a glimpse of what was happening-to make sure that Gray was okay. The man she'd been introduced to as

Blinston kept her moving quickly up the metal stairs to the open door of the plane. "Almost there."

As soon as they were inside, he shut the door, and activated the locking mechanism, then shot her a cheerful smile. "Safe as a bug in a rug. Grab a seat and I'll check you out."

A little shell shocked, Hannah repeated, "Check me out?"

"Over here, I think."

Pointing to a wide leather seat, he indicated she sit. Hannah planted her butt. The jet was luxuriously appointed, modern, lots of tan leather and polished burl tables. The soft leather seat was as comfortable as her sofa at home. And it was *quiet* inside the plane. For the first time in hours she let the tightness seep out of her shoulders and neck.

"I'm Mike by the way. I'll feed you in a minute, but let's check that blood sugar so we know where we are."

Hannah gave a half laugh. "Trust me. I haven't known where the hell I've been all night. I think I fell down a rabbit hole the second I landed in Ecuador, and popped up in some other dimension."

Opening a large first aid box that had been on the table between the seats when she sat down, he took out a monitor. "Well, you're in good hands." Then gestured to her hand. "Finger?"

He motioned to a small bottle of orange juice. Hannah picked up the bottle, holding out her other hand so he could swab her finger with alcohol. Gesturing to his ear, he indicated he was listening to someone else. Hannah was used to it by now. As he listened, eyes twinkling, he used a small glucose meter with a lancet to draw a small drop of blood from her fingertip.

"Yes, Gray," Mike said into his communication device, as he inserted the test strip into the meter, then smiled as he showed her the result was a low 70. A lot higher than it had been before the quick infusion of sugar. She sipped the juice.

"I have her. Yes. Unharmed. She just tested pretty good under the circumstances, and I'm about to feed her. Yes. I will. No, I won't. Don't you have anything better to do than bug us? Out."

She smiled back, when he shook his head. Clearly amused by Grayson's comment. "I agreed to take excellent care of you. And I will not flirt or otherwise encroach on his territory."

"He didn't ask that." Doubting Gray said anything of the sort, Hannah's foolish heart still did a happy little thump. He'd never stake a claim, and certainly not to a colleague. "The Coke helped. I must have you to thank for that."

"You have *Gray* to thank for it," Mike wrapped a blood pressure cuff around her upper arm and started the procedure. "He radioed in the need before I landed." He removed the cuff. "Bit high, 150 over 90. There's a bedroom, a change of clothes, and a decent shower back there. We won't be wheels up for a while. Why don't you grab a quick shower. How do you like your steak?"

"You're a doctor, a chef *and* a pilot?"

"Well," he grinned, "I'm only really qualified to fly. But the other two come in handy more often than not. And I've never had anyone complain about my first aid skills, or my cooking."

Sobered by the reminder of what Gray did every day, and the reality of the necessity for someone with sound medical knowledge around at all times, Hannah pushed out of the comfortable seat. "Thanks, Mike. Really. Well, please. I won't take long-" She glanced out of the small windows, but saw only blackness.

"Take your time, I won't prep until you come out. In the meantime, I'll keep my comm open so I can report the latest updates to you. Good?"

"Perfect."

Hannah made her way to the back of the aircraft. The jet would seat about twelve people comfortably. She hoped Gray wasn't thinking of cramming all the people in the hangar onto this one small plane. "Not my problem." Pushing open the door into a rear cabin, she noted twin beds. On one, neatly folded, was a pile of black fabric. Clothing she presumed. Mike was certainly prepared.

What was happening in the hangar? Why had she heard gunshots- *Stop right there! Not my problem!* "In fact," Hannah said out loud as she circumvented the foot of a bed to get to the bathroom. "From now on, I refuse to take on *anyone* else's freaking problems, but my own- Wow. Pretty snazzy for spies!" The bathroom was small, but luxuriously appointed. Black and cream. Masculine and elegant at the same time. Lots of money spent here. She cranked on the jets.

"And this time next. . .*soon*, I'll *have* no problems! Woohoo, and yay, me." Stripping, and avoiding looking at herself in the mirror over the fancy black sink, she stepped into the pounding spray. The massage jets pummeled her back as she leaned her forehead against the creamy mosaic tiled wall with a sigh of pure relief.

She stayed in the shower long after she should have gotten out. For a few minutes she was in a bubble of. . .*blank*. Getting out meant dealing with whatever she had to deal with. She would.

In a few more minutes.

Unfortunately, the water started getting cold, and being the practical woman that she was, she knew she couldn't hide-stay in there forever. As she stepped *out* of the shower, Grayson stepped *into* the bathroom.

Wearing an impressive erection and an inscrutable expression, he looked like an all you can eat buffet. Six three of tanned, satiny skin, clearly defined, rock hard muscles, and lightly furred chest. Droplets of water sparkled on his short hair and broad shoulders like tiny diamonds.

He'd also taken a shower. But not with her.

"How did you get in?" She steeled herself, but her body had other ideas. Her body loved looking at Grayson's body. A lot. It responded as if his erection, and her girl parts, were joined by an electrical current. Her nerves thrummed and her heart went into over-drive. "I locked the door."

"I have superior lock picking skills."

"Or a key," she said dryly. Since they were both naked, it seemed redundant to pick up her towel.

Narrow eyed, she gave him a hard look. She did not fiddle, or try to cover herself. He'd seen it all a thousand times anyway, as she gave him a firm, "No way, Grayson James Burke." It was not unequivocal. But he had to discover that for himself, and he'd have to work hard for a yes. Not only did he owe that to her, damn it, she deserved him to fight for her, even if the adversary was herself.

"No?"

She wanted him; wanted his hands all over her again, wanted his hardness driving deep inside her. "It's been a long freaking day. I haven't recovered from the last heartbreak you caused me, and frankly I can't handle a double whammy, I really can't. And if you want me, you'll have to do a hell of a lot more than show up late to the party naked."

His penis leaped against his belly, but he stayed where he was, simply looking at her. A drip of water trailed down her shoulder, and over her breast. Hannah gave him a belligerent glare. "*What*?"

"You're even more beautiful than my dreams." His attention stayed on her face as she felt the drop hang on the very tip of her nipple.

"You're delusional." But her heart did a foolish little trip anyway. Years of loving this man hadn't disappeared, just been masked by anger and pain. Hannah wanted those halcyon days back with an ache that hurt her heart all over again. "I have no butt, and my boobs are too small." She heard her mother's voice prompting in her head- *just say 'thank you'*. "And I have cellulite."

His smile, the warm, loving smile she knew and loved, made her heart do calisthenics. "Tink, I've seen every glorious streamlined inch of you, and as a connoisseur, I assure you, you are *prime* from the top of your head to your crooked baby toe." Sobering, his eyes searched her face. "How do you feel?"

Tempted. "Ready to go home. Now, if you'll get out of my way, Mike left me some cl-"

Holding her eyes, he stepped forward, slid his hand around her waist and jerked her body flush against his. Skin to skin. Heat to heat. A half scream was all she managed before he crushed his mouth on hers.

TWELVE

The kiss, rough, hot and hungry, instantly fired up her own needs to a fever pitch. She tasted coffee. He'd had time for a cup between saving the world from the bad guys and displaying himself before her like a smorgasbord.

His mouth took her from zero to a hundred and sixty in about two seconds. Every thought, every doubt in Hannah's mind, evaporated in the heat of the kiss as he lifted her onto the counter.

Having her shower-warmed butt placed on a cold marble countertop was a shock. Eyes narrowed, Hannah pulled her mouth from his, slapped a hand on his chest, and wedged her knee between them. Then shifted to hold him off with a bare foot planted on the hard steps of his six pack. "If this happens, you're mine."

His muscles flexed against her toes in response, and it was to his advantage that he kept his eyes on her face, not her crotch.

Wrapping his hand around her foot, Gray used his thumb to massage her instep, then ran his palm up her leg, shifted her planted foot, so her leg wrapped around his waist as he stepped forward. Holding her gaze, he murmured, "Don't ever doubt it," against her mouth.

Hannah wrapped her arms around his neck, gripping his back with her short nails as he poised the blunt tip of his penis to the entrance of her body. It was delicious feeling them naked skin to naked skin. His hardness to her softness. Everything she wanted was right here in her arms.

"God. Hannah—" Plunging his fingers through her wet hair, he cradled her head as he kissed her as if he'd die if he didn't. He pushed her dripping hair behind her shoulders, then he traced her collar bone with his thumb as he lavished his attention on her mouth. Breath ragged, he glided his hand around her waist, then cupped one cheek in his broad palm.

His fingers skimmed lower to cup her breast. Her nipple, painfully engorged, begged for the attention he lavished on it.

With a groan, Hannah threw back her head as he bent to suckle, pulling a whimper from her constricted throat as his hot breath fanned her damp skin. His low triumphant growl vibrated across her skin like ripples on a brook.

The pulse and jump of his erection pressed at the entrance to her sex, and she shifted eagerly to have him inside her.

Jerking her mouth from his, damp lips throbbing and swollen she shifted closer to the edge of the counter.

Frustrated, she trailed her finger down the arrow of dark hair to the jut of his penis. She ran her fingers over the hard, satiny length of him, loving the hot, smooth feel of his skin. Transferring the bead of moisture she found on the tip, she glided her hand beneath to cup the velvety pouch, cradling him in her hand. "Are you going to do something with this? Or have your forgotten how?"

"It's a fourteen hour flight, give or take." She felt his smile against her throat. "I'm pacing myself."

Goosebumps roughened her skin as he licked a fiery path around the outer shell of her ear, then nibbled his way down her neck to the manic pulse at the base of her throat. Voice ragged, she could barely form the words. "Damnit, Gray! Pace yourself *later*!"

He smiled, gliding his fingers over her rib cage, made a brief detour to explore her navel, then skimmed, feather-light and maddening, over her hip. His light touch wrenched a moan from her, half longing, half frustration. Gray slid a finger into the seam where her leg met her body, his pinky barely brushing her pubic hair. "You love foreplay."

The taut pull of pleasure made her crazy, and she grabbed his wrist as he traced the damp slit of her vulva with an infuriatingly light touch that made her shudder and suck in a breath. "Not when I've waited three frigging *years* for this! Do me *now*, Grayson James Burke!"

That elicited a surprised bark of laughter and a raised brow. "*Do* you?"

"Fuck me?"

"Oh, trust me," his eyes, gleaming with lust and laughter shone like pewter. "I will. Here? Or would you prefer the bed?" Slowly he stroked her damp heat with the blunt tip of his rock hard erection as he spoke. Teasing her until she wiggled and shifted, growling like some kind of feral beast when she didn't get what she wanted. With an annoying, if strained smile, he tightened his arms around her.

"*Here,*" she gasped, barely able to get the words out. "Then on the bed. Then on the floor, than against the wal-" Hannah arched as he gripped her butt in both hands, lifting her to press her down the length of that hardness, until she felt him slide deep inside. Sharp pleasure radiated through her as he filled her to the hilt. Stretched muscles clenched, and her body shook as she adjusted to feel him exactly where she wanted him. She was one hot, aching pulsation of need.

"God," he groaned, breathless, voice tight. "You feel fucking incredible." He sank his teeth into the cords of her neck, his fingers merciless on the muscles of her ass as he pumped into her.

She couldn't answer; all she could do was shut her eyes, ride inner tremors and wait for the building tsunami. Panting with the effort, she moved faster as he clasped her ass. The small pain of his relentless grip melding into the intense sensations as his hips slammed against her inner thighs with a vengeance

She gasped; a high , sharp sound as the first wave of pleasure broke over her. She came hard, moaning as each swell slammed into her, making her clench, and shudder. This was more than a sexual relief that she'd been without for so long, it was an emotional cleansing. Still, it shocked the hell out of her when she suddenly burst into tears.

Still moving inside her, Grayson cupped her face, wiping at the flood with fingers that shook, as he whispered brokenly, "God, Hannah-"

This was beyond words, beyond even conscious thought. It was an avalanche of emotions. The years without him, the high emotions of the day, it was having him in her arms and a succession of amazing multiple O's. Sweat joined the tears, she gasped as the coiling need ratcheted up again before she'd fully recovered from the last climax. Impossible to breathe. Tightening her arms around his neck, she buried her damp face against his throat.

He pumped faster.

"Wait, wait, wait," she pleaded, tightening her arms around his shoulders, the sensation as it built, pleasure so sharp and exquisite she didn't think she could handle more. She needed to come down before she was taken up again. Every nerve in her body pulsed and throbbed, her inner muscles clenched around his hard spar.

He knew to ignore her plea, and his fingers scored her butt as he lifted her, then urged her down onto him again and again, sinking into her deeper, harder. Her muscles shook as she locked her ankles in the small of his back. Thrusting into her faster, he picked up the pace until they were both breathing hard, skin slick with sweat. He lifted her higher, then thrust harder, a hot juicy slide of intense pleasure that made her come again.

Back arched, she clasped his length more tightly within her vaginal walls, moving with him as they rose and fell. Hannah splayed her hands on the shifting muscles of his back, hanging on for the ride. Everything disappeared. All she could do was feel. The hot ache inside her torqued tighter and tighter as Gray controlled the movement of her body so that she fell when he thrust, and rose when he withdrew. It was like dancing. Perfect synchronization.

He knew exactly how to keep the tension high, how to sustain that almost peak that kept her on edge, begging for more. Every thrust, every parry, connected muscles, tendons and nerves, like a direct electrical current, to her nipples, her skin, her eyes, her arched throat.

The lights were low as he carried her into the room, and followed her down on the bed, still deep inside her. Pushing her wet hair off her face he traced her cheek, then her chin. "You know I'm yours, have *always* been yours. Heart. Body,

Soul. There hasn't been a day that's gone by, from the first moment I saw you skating down my driveway in that pink fairy getup, to the day I was the oldest guy at your senior prom, that I haven't loved you. *Loved* you, fallen *in* love with you. Loved you when we were apart.

"Then-"

He kissed her, then flipped her while her brain was fuzzy, her lips throbbed, and her muscles were still clenching around him. Sitting astride Gray was a favorite position. She punished him by digging her nails into the light covering of hair on his chest. Rising and falling slowly enough to give him a turn at measured torment. Hannah knew exactly where and how to touch him. Knew what made him crazy, knew when to slow down and when to speed up.

"Killing me!" His chest rose and fell with his erratic breathing, his large hands hard on her hips as he thrust up as she plunged down.

Sweat ran into her eye, and the taut pull of pleasure surged through her as each stoke went deeper. "You. Love. It."

"Love. *You*! Jesus, woman. Like tha-*Yes*!"

Hannah spun off into a brilliant fireworks display as she came hard. Grayson's body went rigid beneath her and he yelled her name.

Gasping, limp and satiated, Hannah collapsed on his chest, burying her face against his damp neck, as their skin stuck together. Every muscle in her body had turned to sensitized liquid. She gave a shuddering sigh as he straightened out her legs to make her more comfortable, although Hannah could've slept right where she was.

"Hmm." she realized the jet was bumping and shimming down the runway. "How many people are crammed on this plane?" Hannah imagined them six deep in the main cabin. All knowing she was in here naked.

"You. Me. Mike."

It was a relief knowing there weren't dozens of people out there knowing what they were up to back here. She propped herself up on her folded arms, braced on his chest. "Are you done with all your spy stuff?"

"For now, yeah." Lazily he stroked his palm down her back. "Without you, we would never have fingered Stonefish."

Hannah pulled a face. "That's a nasty way of putting it. But that's great."

She almost jumped a foot at the disembodied voice over an intercom. "Hurry up kids, we have places to go and things to do."

"Holy crap!" she dropped her voice to a whisper. "Can he hear us?"

"No. But he'll know if we don't have our belts buckled before he takes off."

"We better get dressed before we go out there, don't you think?"

Grayson picked up a strap and buckle from the side of the bed. "Right here."

"Seriously?" Hannah gave an inelegant snort of laughter. "You want to strap me to a bed?"

"Mike won't lift off otherwise."

She rolled off him to lie by his side. "What kind of kinky stuff goes on back here?"

He grinned. "The belt's used if we have an injured operative. Lie down again, my skeptical little fairy."

"We have the all clear from the tower," Mike's voice came over the PA. "Buckle up, love birds. Wheels up in five."

"Told you. Hand me the strap on your side. There." He buckled, and tightened the belt across their waists.

She looked at the wide strap across their naked bodies. "Do you see how ridiculous this is?"

He turned his head on the pillow they shared. "I don't know. I kinda like it." His wet hair brushed her forehead.

"Did you take a shower?"

"There's another bathroom in the main cabin."

"We don't smell of soap."

"An operative isn't supposed to smell pretty. Imagine a bad guy smelling Brut as he rounds a corner. We're supposed to not have a smell at all."

"Hmm.

"But *your* skin has a deliciously, distinct smell. Honey and orange blossoms. I could find you blindfolded in a dark room."

"Yeah, you mentioned that before. But that's not likely to come up soon, since I live in Chicago, and I have no idea where you live. What happened with Colton?"

"My brother's on his way to Montana, which is where *I* happen to live, in the second transport. He's not a happy camper, but considering how I was feeling when I left him, he's lucky he has no more than a black eye and a split lip."

The wheels bit into the gravel as they increased speed, shifting Hannah flush against Gray, so their arms touched. His bicep flexed in response to the brush of her skin. She loved the way he just tossed out a pertinent piece of information in-between the rest.

She rolled a little on her side so her breast pressed against his arm.

His muscles bunched everywhere they touched. She raised a brow, something he'd taught her when she was twelve. "You beat up your own brother?"

"Once, for putting you in danger, once for stealing from the Moms," he paused, eyes hot as he scanned her features. "And once, for taking you on board that fucking ship so he could show off."

When she dropped her gaze to his mouth, her own lips pulsed in response. "You hit him for the same reason *twice*."

"Only because Hensley held me back," his tone was dry.

"Don't sound so proud of yourself! *You* stole a hangar, *and* three fishing boats, and you berated your brother? You two are a fine frigging pair, aren't you?"

"One does what one has to do."

"Yes. You Burke boys always did do whatever you damn-well pleased, didn't you? Just so you know, as soon as I get this last matter resolved, I'm moving to an undisclosed tropical beach, where there are hot and cold running waiters, no telephones, and clothing is optional." As she added the last, she had the satisfaction of seeing his pupils flare.

He didn't reach for her. He didn't attempt to close the scant few inches between their mouths. His expression was dark and serious, his gray eyes glittered like polished silver. "What about your dream of being a performer?"

There was no chance of that now, probably never had been a chance, only a dream. She'd grown up. Moved on. Dreamed less, and become a pragmatist. "I'll wear my bikini and play for the beachcombers. What do you care?"

"I care-"

The plane lifted off as they lay side by side, a belt across their waists. Tying them together, when, despite the mind blowing sex, emotionally they were miles and years apart. Hannah stared up at the ceiling, tears stinging her lids. "If I hadn't been in Ecuador chasing after Colton, I'd never have seen you again, would I? Not a damn word in three years, Gray. I guess you figured I wouldn't notice your absence for another three, or thirty! The odds of us bumping into each other in Ecuador of all places must be – Oh, a breath over zero to zero."

"Zero was all we needed."

A twist of fate that neither could've anticipated. Knowing now what Gray did for a living, made the chance meeting more profound and precious.

She swallowed over the emotions knotted in her throat. If she believed in fate. . .

She didn't. Not anymore. Grayson's betrayal three years ago had brought her back to reality from the fairytales with a resounding thump.

He'd broken her heart once, but she couldn't let this opportunity pass without letting him know she'd never stopped loving him. Asshole that he was.

Then she'd finally be able to set them both free.

It was going to be a second blow to her still cracked heart she wasn't sure she'd recover from. But if she didn't do this or face this, it would always haunt her. *He* would haunt her. As he always had. God. . . Her chest ached and her eyes burned.

She felt the wheels of the aircraft retract as the plane reached altitude. "How long's the flight?"

"Fourteen hours give or take with refueling."

She unsnapped the buckle. "Are you allowed to use electronic devices on this fancy plane of yours?"

"Su- Absolutely not."

"Right answer." She touched his unshaven jaw. He shuddered, closing his eyes as she traced his features lightly with one finger, then trailed a line from his stubborn jaw down the center of his chest.

"Because I don't want to have to figure out who you're talking to when you're with me. And I don't want you talking to anyone *but* me for the next fourteen hours."

"I'm your prisoner?"

Her lips curled into a smile as she glanced down at the seatbelt. "Yes. Do you need a hostage negotiator?"

"If you're planning on keeping me as your love slave for fourteen hours you're all I need."

"Another right answer."

THIRTEEN

G ray stacked his hands under his head to watch her get dressed. She insisted on being clothed before they went into the main cabin to forage for something to eat. Mike had two juicy steaks with their names on them, just waiting to hit the broiler.

He admired Hannah's pale butt, taut from her yoga classes. "You have a Grade A ass, you know that?" Grayson said lazily, enjoying the view. Golden hair a tangled mess around her shoulders, her creamy skin reddened in patches from his rough beard, she looked like a well satiated pagan goodness standing there naked.

Glancing at him over her shoulder she pulled black drawstring pants over her bare butt and reached for a long-sleeved t-shirt- also black. "You sweet-talking devil you. Hurry up and at least put pants on. Feed me. I have to eat to keep up my strength for the rest of the flight."

He'd rather keep her in bed, but they both needed fuel. Reluctantly he flung his feet to the floor, and stood. Since his LockOut was in the other bathroom, he walked across to a hidden set of drawers to dig out an identical outfit to the one Hannah wore.

He knew as soon as he heard her horrified inhalation, that she'd just got a visual of the horrific scars on his back. Burns, whip slashes.*Stonefish's legacy.*

"Dear God," she whispered, horror thick in her voice. "Who did that to you?"

He turned. He hadn't wanted her to get a look at the worst of it. Stonefish was known for his secondhand cruelty. Never lifted a hand himself, but tortured through his intermediaries while he watched from a remote location. He was a sadistic son of a bitch, and Grayson suspected the men sent to work him over in that shoe-box-sized Columbian cell had added their own brutal twists to the interrogation.

"Stonefish. Indirectly- Oh, Jesus. Don't cry, sweetheart. It was a long time ago."

Rushing into his arms, she wrapped her arms around his waist, her tears hot on his chest. "It's happening *today* for me."

Grayson stroked her back murmuring soft words that made no sense, but seemed to calm her. Knowing his beautiful, delicate Tink had been *that* close to the sadistic fucker chilled Grayson's blood.

"I want you to share every last horrific detail with me." Her arms tightened. "But will you tell me, as briefly, and with as *little* detail as possible, so I know *now*?"

"I was on an op in Columbia. Captured a few weeks before returning home for our wedding. His people wanted information on what T-FLAC knew about the ALNF— For almost six months they kept me isolated in the mountains. Torture. Mind Games. *Hell*." He didn't want to downplay what he'd endured. Better she know now. "It was- bad. Real bad.

But my men found me and broke me out. It took the better part of a year in the hospital and rehab-"

"You'd just been released from the hospital that night you came to see me? God, Gray! Why didn't you tie me down and force me to listen to you?"

"Not exactly *released.*" He kissed her tears away. "I saw you kissing some guy that afternoon, then my mother told me you'd met- Fuck, no that's not it. Or rather all of it. Yeah, I was jealous. And under better circumstances, I would've gone in there and ripped the guy's face off and staked my claim. But a moment of sanity prevailed. I knew, as much as it broke me to admit it to myself, that you deserved more than what I'd become. I was broken, Tink. Emotionally and physically. I didn't want to accept it, but that was my reality."

"I would've accepted you any way I got you." Liquid blue eyes shone up at him. "I loved you unconditionally, Grayson. Then, and even more so now. Don't ever doubt that."

A shudder went through his body as he shook off the lingering fear that she'd reject him out of hand. But this was Hannah- "I knew. It kept me going when things turned to shit. But I couldn't inflict the man I'd become on you. I loved you too much. I would've destroyed everything good in you. That's why it was best for me to fuck off and work on myself a while longer. You deserved a whole man. Not half of one." He buried his nose in her still damp hair, swearing he could smell orange blossoms. "Stopping Stonefish has been my holy grail, my reason for moving through my days. He eluded me for three years, on four continents- Now he's not only identified, but in T-FLAC's hands. He won't escape. He's over. That impediment to our happiness is. . .over."

"Over?" Drenched eyes haunted, she shook her head. "How could it be? He's wrapped up, but the world is *filled* with terrorists. You know better than I do, there are always more. And I know you, Gray. You'll always want to be in the thick of things. As soon as this is over, you'll be on to your next assignment."

"*You* are my next assignment, Hannah."

"That's nice to hear, but hardly practical." She stepped out of his arms to pull on the T-shirt. It was a crime to cover those perky breasts. "I'm going home to Chicago, and hopefully I'll persuade the Moms to sell the store. You're a spy. How do those two diametrically opposed lives coexist? Even James Bond didn't have a steady girlfriend."

He'd tell her later that the pill Stonefish tried to give his lieutenant, Deeks, was cyanide. That they'd discovered that his feckless brother had stolen a handful of diamonds on his way off the ship. More than his buy in. Hannah could repay the Moms' money three-fold. He'd tell her *all* that- later. Much later.

"I don't want you as my girlfriend. We lost three years. I want us to get married and start our life together right away."

"A rose covered cottage with a sniper rifle over the door? How do you see that working, Gray?"

Operatives *did* marry. It was always a work in progress, but they seemed to make it work. But if Hannah objected, he'd figure something else out. Because nothing, and no one was ever going to keep him away from her again. "I've been considering switching gears, and instructing operatives from our HQ in Montana. That's just a couple of hours plane ride to Chicago. And as much as the Moms travel, they could change locations and buy places near us. I'm not promising easy, but will you come to Montana, marry me, and be my love, Tink?"

Cupping his face in both hands, her big blue eyes scanned his face. Her lips were pink and slightly swollen, and she drew in a small shuddering breath. "It's all about taking risks, about rewards and second chances, isn't it? Nothing ventured, nothing gained. No one will ever love you as much as I do. You've always been my heart, Grayson. Always. That will never change. So, yes, I'll go anywhere with you. Everything else can be figured out as we get to it-"

Grayson wrapped her in his arms, tilting her chin so they were eye to eye. "Yeah. All that." And he kissed her with everything in him. They were going to get that happy ending after all.

THE END

Grayson "Pumice" Burke

AGE: Four years older than Hannah and Colton

PHYSICAL CHARACTERISTICS:
Eyes: Gray
Height: 6' 3"
Hair: Short-cropped, dark
Fit and strong, a hard body
Scars: forehead, horrific scars on his back, thin white scar on corner of mouth
Broad shoulders
Tough, mean and dangerous as hell

FAMILY:
Colton, brother
Michelle Wickham, mother – three times divorced

EMPLOYMENT: T-FLAC Operative

PERSONALITY
& ATTITUDE:
Patience of a saint

QUIRKS &
HABITS:
Nobody cocked an eyebrow like Grayson

WEAPONS:
Glock, Ka-Bar

BACKGROUND:
*He has been trying to catch the head of the Abadinista National Liberation Front, known as Stonefish for the last three years.
*Equated his capture by Stonefish tied to the loss of Hannah
*Left Hannah at the altar

Hannah "Tinker Belle" Endicott

AGE: Same age as Colton
Four years younger than Grayson

PHYSICAL CHARATERISTICS:
Height: 5'4"
Gifted musician
Slender & ethereal
Hair: Shoulder length, streaky honey-blonde, blunt cut
Eyes: Blue
Parents divorced when Hannah was 2. Mother was a flight attendant, then opened an antiques business with Michelle Wickham

FRIENDS:
Grayson Burke "Pumice"
Colton Burke "GQ"

EMPLOYMENT:
Provenance Inc.

PERSONALITY
& ATTITUDE:
People-pleaser

QUIRKS &
HABITS:
Claustrophobia

LIKES:
--knowing what to expect and how to prepare.

DISLIKES:
Secrets

CHILDHOOD:
Ran around with Colton and Grayson Wickham.

HOME:
Chicago

BACKGROUND:
Wanted to be a concert cellist
Diabetic, has to take insulin.
Grayson gave her, her first kiss.
Grayson was her first lover.

Colton "GQ" Burke

AGE: Four years younger than Grayson

PHYSICAL CHARTERISTICS
Height: 6'
Hair: Sandy Blond
Looks like a movie star or a GQ cover model
Booming voice.

FAMILY:
Grayson, brother
Michelle Wickham, mother – three times divorced

PERSONALITY
& ATTITUDE:
All bluff and bravado until he was called out.
Uncomplicated charm and zest for life

BACKGROUND:
*Using the mom's money to buy into a deal and the money is converted to diamonds.
*Hannah, Colton's lifelong friend. She followed him to Equator to get the money back.
*Every time Colton got some wild investment, harebrained opportunity, he went to the moms and used good looks and charm to con them out of a huge sum.

T-FLAC Background
Terrorist Force Logistic Assault Command

Vitute et Armis Fide Mea Semper Frater

By courage and by arms. On my word of honor. Always brothers.

As the Cold War fell to bits of rubble, top level government officials and those in the private sector saw a new breed of organization gain momentum. The major threats no longer hinged on the posturing of super powers. An even more dangerous enemy emerged – small, well funded guerilla groups began to drive fear into the lives of people all over the world. They were rich, connected, quiet, determined and often preferred killing to make their point.

Governments paralyzed by the rule of law and international treaties and conventions required months to react. Because of this, a new industry was born – private anti-terrorist organizations. Premier among them is T-FLAC.

Geoffrey Wright, Lucas Sullivan, and Katrina DeGlaure founded T-FLAC utilizing their connections – political, military and scientific. Headquartered at a sprawling complex in Montana, they recruited and trained the first operatives in the 1980s. T-FLAC specialized in difficult, sticky situations, often hired quietly by officials whose hands were otherwise tied.

Every candidate faced a grueling test of ability, courage, ethics and loyalty. For the safety and integrity of the organization field operatives work in small teams. The identities of operatives is closely held information, shared only on a need-to-know basis. Operatives often go years, even their entire careers - without knowing the identities of the other T-FLAC agents in the organization.

T-FLAC agents know their code by rote. Vitute et armis, Fide mea. Semper Frater. Courage and by arms. On my word of honor. Always brothers.

Agents can be male or female. Young or old. They are your neighbors. Your friends. Your guardians. Protecting the innocent is a calling. Destroying terror wherever it breeds is a mandate.

They are the men and women of T-FLAC.

T-FLAC Mission Statement

Vision: To be the world's leading provider of strategic, logistical and technological solutions while retaining anonymity as individuals.

Mission: Terrorist Force Logistical Assault Command (T-FLAC) effectively and efficiently integrates resources, technology and experience to provide top-level solutions to the most difficult situations. We exceed expectations where others fail. Guided by courage, ingenuity, innovation and a desire for a safer world, T-FLAC professionals utilize state-of-the-art training, innovative technology and logistical solutions to deliver results world-wide. T-FLAC recognizes that in this post-Cold War era, terrorism is the primary threat to democratic principles across the world. Our combat missions are directed at the base of global terror operations. T-FLAC's mission is to eliminate all such threats by all, and any means at our disposal.

T-FLAC Core Values Ethics: For the ancient Greeks, the word meant "character." For Aristotle, the study of ethics was the study of excellence or the virtues of character. It has come to mean the study and practice of the "good life," the kind of life people ought to live.

In our time, the concept of ethics has broadened to include not only the characteristics of the good person, but also the "best practices" in various professions, among them medicine, the law, the military. We are committed to serving, and expect the highest standards of ethical and professional behavior and adherence to a universally accepted core of values from all our employees

Teamwork: There is no "I" in team, just as there is no "I" in T-FLAC. We function as a uniformly coordinated collection of experience and expertise, where all members of the company work to bring about innovation and solutions that serve our mission to the highest degree possible.

Courage: Fear is only that which we have not overcome. In T-FLAC courage is not the absence of fear, but rather the determination that our mission is of more importance than the fear and the resulting strength and focus, which arises from that determination.

Respect: Each member of the team is essential. We give, and expect in return, respect for others, their beliefs, and their unique perspectives and ideas. We realize that like technologically advanced piece of equipment, each element must work with precision, independently, but in unison, to produce precise results.

Innovation: We encourage, appreciate, and seek out the best of the best superior performance in all areas of operations. We recognize that there are always opportunities for improvement and we strive to elevate expectations and exceed in situations that others deem impossible.

Counterterrorism Policy:1. NO negotiation, make no concessions to terrorists.2. Bring terrorists to justice for their crimes no matter who or where they are.3. Isolate and apply pressure on states that sponsor terrorism, forcing them to change their behavior either overtly or covertly.4. Bolster the counterterrorism capabilities of those countries friendly to the mandates of the U.S.5. Improve counterterrorism cooperation with foreign governments and participate in the development, coordination, and implementation of American counterterrorism policy in accordance with the policies of the United States Government.

International Terrorism:

Hostages:

T-FLAC will make no concessions to individuals or groups holding official or private U.S. citizens hostage. Our operatives will use every resource necessary to gain the safe return of American citizens being held hostage. At the same time, it is our policy to deny hostage takers the benefits of ransom, prisoner releases, policy changes, or other acts of concession.

Areas of Expertise:

- Find and retrieve critical personnel and/or property
- Full-range of armaments
- Hard target and soft target risk assessment
- Critical infrastructure assurance
- Physical elimination of terrorist cells
- Homeland and executive security
- Combat/demilitarization
- Nonproliferation/counter-proliferation
- Intelligence
- Private protection of Foreign Dignitaries
- Counterintelligence
- Persons of Special Interest - Snatch and Grab

T-FLAC Covert Operatives

AJ COOPER: Operative - Out of Sight, Hot Ice
ALEX STONE: Operative (PSI Unit) - Edge of Danger, Edge of Darkness
ALEXANDER "LYNX" STONE: Operative - The Mercenary, Hide & Seek
APOLLO HAWKINS: Operative (In Cairo) - Out Of Sight
ARITARIQ: Operative (In Cairo) Out Of Sight
ASH: Operative - On Thin Ice
ASHER DAKLIN: Operative - Hot Ice
AUSTIN: Operative - Hot Ice
BANTHER: (Deceased) Operative - White Heat
BURTON: Operative - Hot Ice
CALEB EDGE: Operative (PSI Unit) - Edge of Danger, Edge of Darkness
CAROL: Nurse - White Heat
CATHERINE SEYMOUR (Savage): Operative & Tango - Hide & Seek, Out Of Sight, and Hot Ice
CHAPMAN: Operative (PSI Unit) - Edge of Darkness
CONNOR JORDAN: Operative (PSI Unit) - Edge of Darkness
CONRAD CHRISTOF: Operative (In Australia) - Out Of Sight
CURTIS: (Deceased): Operative - The Mercenary
CURTNER: Operative & Trainer - Out of Sight
DAAN VILJOEN: Operative - Hot Ice
DARIUS (aka DARE): Operative - Hide & Seek, White Heat
DEKKER: Operative (PSI Unit) - Edge of Fear
DEREK WRIGHT: Operative - On Thin Ice, Out of Sight

DOYLE: Operative (Security Division) - White Heat

DUNCAN EDGE: Operative (PSI Unit) - Edge of Danger, Edge of Fear

FARRIS KEIR: Operative - Edge of Fear

FRANK FISK: Operative - Hot Ice

GABRIEL: Operative - Out Of Sight

GABRIEL EDGE: Operative (PSI Unit) - Edge of Darkness,Edge of Fear

GARDNER: Operative - Hot Ice

GARY LANDIS: Operative (PSI Unit) - Edge of Darkness

GREG SANDOVAL: Operative - White Heat

GUERRERO: Operative - White Heat

HOLLWELL: Operative - Hot Ice

DR. HOWARD: Doctor - White Heat

HUGO CALETTI: (Deceased) Operative - In Too Deep

HUNTINGTON ST. JOHN: Operative - Hot Ice, Kiss & Tell, On Thin Ice, In Too Deep, White Heat

IRIS: Nurse - White Heat

JAKE DOLAN: Operative - Kiss & Tell, Hide & Seek, On Thin Ice, Out of Sight, In Too Deep, Edge of Fear

JOE SKULLESTAD: (Deceased) Operative - Kiss & Tell

JUANITA SALAZAR: Operative (PSI Unit) - Edge of Darkness

KANE WRIGHT: Operative - Out of Sight, In Too Deep, Kiss & Tell, White Heat

KLEIVER: Operative - White Heat

KRISTA DAVIS: (Deceased) Operative - The Mercenary

KURTZ: (Deceased) Operative - White Heat

KYLE WRIGHT: Operative - Hide & Seek, In Too Deep, On Thin Ice, Out of Sight

LARK ORELA: Operative (PSI Unit) - Edge of Danger, Edge of Darkness, Edge of Fear
LEVINE: Operative - White Heat
MANNY ESCOBAR: Operative - Out Of Sight, Hot Ice
MARCUS SAVIN: Operative (Boss/CEO) - The Mercenary, White Heat
MAURO ZAMPIERI: (Deceased) Operative - White Heat
MAX ARIES: Operative - Hot Ice, White Heat
MCBRIDE: Operative - Out Of Sight
MICHAEL WRIGHT: Operative - In Too Deep, On Thin Ice, Kiss & Tell, Hide & Seek, Out of Sight
DR. MICHAEL YET: Doctor (HQ) - White Heat
MICHAELS: (Deceased) Operative - The Mercenary
MIKE RAGUSA: Operative (Security Division) - White Heat
NATASHA: Laundry (HQ) - White Heat
NAVARRO (Rafael): Operative - Hot Ice, White Heat, Ice Cold
NEAL BISHOP: Operative - Hot Ice
NIIGATA (Keiko): (Deceased) Operative - White Heat
NOAH HART: Operative (PSI Unit) - Edge of Darkness
PAUL BRITTON: (Deceased) Operative - Kiss & Tell
PAUL ROBERTS: Operative (Co-Pilot) - Hot Ice
PETER BLAINE: (Deceased) Operative (PSI Unit) - Edge of Darkness
PIET COATZEE: (Deceased) Operative - Hot Ice
RAYNARD ACKART: Operative - White Heat
REBECCA SANTOS: Tech girl - White Heat
RICHARD STRUBEN: (Deceased) Operative - Out of Sight
RIFKIN: Mailroom (Operative Trainee) - White Heat
ROMAN KILLIAN: Operative (In Cairo) - Out of Sight

ROSS LERMA: (Deceased) Operative (& Tango = Dancer) - Kiss & T   ell

SAM PLUNKETT: (Deceased) Operative - Kiss & Tell

SAUL TANNENBAUM: Tech guy (Encryption Dept.) - White Heat

SAVAGE (CATHERINE SEYMOUR): Operative (& Tango) - Hide & Seek, Out Of Sight, Hot Ice

SEBASTIAN TREMAYNE: Operative - Edge of Danger, Edge of Darkness

SIMON PARRISH: Operative (PSI Unit) - Edge of Danger, Edge of Darkness

STAN BROWN: Operative (PSI Unit) - Edge of Darkness

TATE: Operative - Hot Ice

TAYLOR KINCAID: Operative - Hot Ice, White Heat

TES WONDWESEN: Operative (In Cairo) Out Of Sight

THOM LINDLEY: (Deceased) Operative (PSI Unit) - Edge of Danger, Edge of Darkness

TONY (Anthony) ROOK: Operative - Edge of Fear

UPTON FITZGERALD: Operative (PSI Unit) -Edge of Danger, Edge of Darkness

YANCY: Operative (PSI Unit) - Edge of Danger, Edge of Darkness

Cherry Adair Interview

Questions with New York Times & USA Today's Bestselling Author Cherry Adair

1. **What is the best part of being a writer? What is the worst?**

The people I create can't tell me "No!" lol I love writing the second (3rd, 4th, 5th lol) draft. For me, writing the first draft is like building a house half a brick at a time with one arm tied behind my back and a blindfold on! Slow and painful. Unfortunately, at this stage of the process I have the attention span of a water newt, and can't seem to sit still for more than 15 agonizing minutes at a time. But once the walls are up, I'm filled with gusto, and then I'm obsessive about getting all the finish work done. Once a decorator, always a decorator.

I love the process of polishing and rewriting. I love the minutia of the last tweak, that last spit polish before sending it off to my editor. I even love revisions from my editor, because that gives me yet another shot at making the book shine.

B. What is the worst?

That first draft. Erk! Not my fave. And having to be disciplined. It's hard on an Aries to plant her behind in that chair. I love to write, but sometimes the process of sitting down to write is painful.

2. Why do you write?

I can't. . .not. If I didn't get it all down on paper the voices in my head would mean I was crazy instead of creative.

CHERRY ADAIR

3. Name one eye-opening thing you've learned from your book research.

Snakes have two penises. (peni?) Not something that comes up in the normal course of conversation that often. (book: BLACK MAGIC)

4. Do you have a favorite motto?

Two. I love Mark Twain's: My books are like water; those of the great geniuses are wine. (Fortunately) everybody drinks water. And Gary Player's: -The harder you work, the luckier you get.

5. Do you have a favorite fictional hero? Favorite fictional heroine?

I'm pretty fickle. Whichever character I'm wring at the time is always my favorite. I must admit though that I do have a soft spot for Marc Savin (The Mercenary) because he was my first hero. We always remember our first. I'm mad about Gideon Stark in GIDEON. He's the brother of Zak Stark (HUSH) I couldn't wait to see what really happened to him in the jungle when he and his brother separated after the kidnapping. And for much of the book, he doesn't know who he is or how he ended up where he ended up. SO much fun to write. I love writing jungle books (HIDE & SEEK, NIGHT FALL, TROPICAL HEAT, HUSH AND GIDEON. So far. Lol) I love exotic locals because to me the location is as much a character as my people.

As for a heroine, I adored Teal Williams in UNDERTOW. She was such a great foil for Zane, I've never written a

119

heroine who is shy and unkept. lol. It was fascinating to get into her skin and figure out how she ticked.

6. Which fictional character would you hang out with?

Any of my heroes. (Not necessarily at the same time. Lol)

7. What is one of your favorite book covers, your own or someone else's?

I love the cover of WHIRLPOOL - Him- the watery colors- him- the puzzled look on his face -him- his abs - oh, yes, Finn.

8. What would readers be surprised to learn about you?

I'm pretty much an open book, so probably not much. I used to be an Interior Designer, I'm originally from Cape Town, South Africa. I love to read, enjoy playing in my garden (preferable after someone else has done the sweaty work) and have to write every day. Spare time? What spare time?!

9. What's the strangest thing you've ever learned by Googling your name?

I'm a stripper. A fruit. A rude connotation A blossom. And a bomb. lol

10. If you could go backward or forward in time which would you chose? Why?

Back, because I'd know what was coming next.

11. Are you a plotter or a pantser?

Plotter. I plot extensively and have a method called Plotting By Color which uses Post-It notes by the truck-load (3-M loves me) My PLOTTING BY COLOR book will be available next Summer.

12. You are a fierce advocate, and mentor, to new authors, how do you find the time?

I make the time because I love helping and motivating new authors, and authors who are in a writing slump. I have several FB pages devoted to all things new authors (BICC Butt In Chair Challenge) Everyone is welcome.

13. Are there discussion guides available for your books? Also, do you participate in author phone chats? And if so, how would my readers go about scheduling one?

Yes, each book has a discussion guide available. Me, talk? Of course! (see above re: moderation)! I love talking with readers. The best way for you to get the discussion guides or arrange phone chats, or workshops is to contact me at Adairsupport@msn.com

14. When did you start your writing career?

Long before I published. I wrote (and shredded) 17 books before The Mercenary came out in 1993

15. Since you live in the Northwest, where do you get your inspiration? Do you travel to the places in your books?

I have traveled to many of the exotic locals in my books, but not all of them. I don't like creepy-crawlies or not being anywhere near a shower or a flushing toilet! (and observant readers will notice that my heroines don't like the same things)

16. What other type of research do you do in order to start a book? Especially with the black ops elements in your T-FLAC series?

I do extensive research - it's one of the most time consuming, and fun, aspects of writing for me. I'm lucky enough to have fans and friends in interesting places who fill me in on some of the local color first hand. When I'm doing research I try to find an expert in that field who is usually happy to answer all my question. Over the years I've made a lot of fascinating contacts because of my writing. (and a few very scary people, too!) I know several black ops guys who are incredibly monosyllabic in their answers, and it's like pulling hens teeth to get any kind of direct information out them. But once they got what I was writing, and that not only didn't I need to know troop movement in Iraq (or wherever, I really didn't want to know classified Intel) they were great at giving me other interesting factoids to make my operatives fun and interesting.

I met an interesting Ph.D nuclear physicist who helped me with info in CHAMELEON. A Venezuelan "business man" who loves my books, and has offered to help me with whatever I need (Let's leave it at that. Lol) Jacques Cousteau's grandson, Fabien Cousteau (who is as yummy and delish as one of my heroes!) has helped with research for several of my books over the years. And I found a fascinating treasure hunter named Dr. Lubos Kordac who is helping me with details on salvaging for the Cutter Cay books. I've collected a fascinating little black book filled with incredible and invaluable contacts. If I told you where I hide it I'd have to have one of my heroes (talk!!??) to you.

17. Will you continue to write T-FLAC novels?

I love my T-FLAC operatives, and yes, I will write them as long as readers love them as much as I do. My latest book is WHILPOOL which is the last in the Cutter Cay trilogy (this trilogy has 6 books. Math is my Super Power. lol) is about deep sea treasure hunters and were a blast to write. Now I'm plotting the new T-FLAC novel which will be called Absolute Honor -the second in my new Fallen Agents of T-FLAC trilogy (following Absolute Doubt)

18. Do you have a favorite character you've written?

I'm pretty fickle. Whichever character I'm wring at the time is always my favorite. I must admit though that I do have a soft spot for Marc Savin (The Mercenary) because he was my first hero. We always remember our first.

19. Who do you read? Favorite authors?

I used to read a book a day. Now I'm lucky if I have time to finish a book in a month! That's the downside of doing what I do. I love being an author, but it's left me no time to enjoy one of my greatest pleasures. Some of my fave authors in no particular order – Gina Showater, Shannon McKenna, Nora Roberts. . . and dozens of others.

20. I know you like to take walks, what else do you do in your spare time?

I don't like to take walks! <g> I walk because it's good for me, and gets me away from my computer for a bit of fresh air with the dogs. Lol And what spare time? When I'm not writing/researching/editing/day dreaming I have fun with readers on my Facebook, and Twitter pages.

21. What's your contact info?

I love hearing from readers through my web site www.cherryadair.com (where you can see pictures of all my heroes, read excerpts from my books, and find my complete booklist.) I'm always on Facebook and Twitter and my e mail is adairsupport@msn.com

About Cherry Adair

Libraries, Love, and Happily Ever After

I grew up in a suburb of Cape Town (South Africa) with a wonderful library. The building was over a hundred years old, two stories, with a sweeping mahogany staircase leading up to the second floor. No one under 13 was allowed up those stairs. No exceptions.

In the Children's Library I read my way through every book, short story, piece of loose paper, envelope, or shopping list used as bookmarks, I was ready to go upstairs. MORE than ready!

On my thirteenth birthday the best present from my mother was a brand new library card. I burst into tears, I was so happy. That year, my birthday fell on a Sunday. Talk about bad timing! Worse, the library was closed on Monday's. I had ants in my pants, and a list as long as my arm of the books I would check out the second I walked through those double, mahogany doors on the second floor. But I had to wait 48 long, anticipatory, hours.

On Tuesday morning, my parents (yes, my father actually took the morning off work for this momentous occasion, and they allowed me to go to school late because, for goodness sake! I could not possibly have waited until 3:30!) and I waited in the car outside for the doors to open at nine. I had, of course, been wide awake and bushytailed since 5 A.M.

When the heavy, carved door opened, the three of us were standing there in the pouring rain. I didn't care. I would have dashed through the first crack as the door was unlocked and pulled open. OMG! It opened so slooooowly!

My heart started pounding so hard, I gripped my Mom's hand in case I fainted before I got upstairs. I have never in my life been that excited, and filled with quite that much anticipation as that day. (Not even on my Honeymoon – but that's another story.)

With my parents on either side of me, I stood at the base of those sweeping, mahogany stairs, frozen in my tracks, savoring the moment. I'd waited so long for this I could hardly breathe. The treads were worn from over a hundred years of feet going up and down them. The swooping gracefully curved banister was satiny smooth (I knew, because I'd been stroking the bottom curve of it for years as I looked up longingly) from thousands of hands (and probably bottoms) sliding down it.

My father crooked his elbow in a sweetly gallant gesture which I've never forgotten. I slipped my hand around his arm, and together, the three of us ascended.

My memory has a choir of angels singing on the top landing, and white doves swooping overhead, but I'm pretty sure the Rondebosch Public Library would have frowned on singing and bird poop, so it probably didn't happen that way.

When we reached the top of the stairs, taken in complete and reverent silence, my father reached over and pushed opened the double doors.

The smell hit me first. Paper. Leather. Dust. Books. Adventure. Romance. I had to just stand there and take it in. THEN I gave my Librarian The List.

Number One: Gone With The Wind. Ahhhhh Bliss. Loved and hated Scarlett, and started writing the moment I closed that book. I rewrote the end many, many times(It was only years, and maturity, later that I knew the ending was absolutely perfect.)

I've been a romance writer ever since. It's the best job in the world and I can't imagine doing anything else.

Always an adventurer in life as well as writing, New York Times best-selling author Cherry Adair moved halfway across the globe from Cape Town, South Africa to the United States in her early years to become an interior designer. She started what eventually became a thriving interior design business. "I loved being a designer because it was varied and creative, and I enjoyed working with the public." A voracious reader when she was able to carve out the time, Cherry found her brain crowded with characters and stories of her own.

"Eventually," she says, "the stories demanded to be told." Now a resident of the Pacific Northwest she shares the award-winning adventures of her fictional T-FLAC counter terrorism operatives with her readers. When asked why she chooses to write romantic action adventure, she says, "Who says you can't have adventure and a great love life? Of course if you're talking about an adventurous love life, that's another thing altogether. I write romantic suspense coupled with heart-pounding adventure because I like to entertain, and nothing keeps readers happier than a rollercoaster read, followed by a happy ending."

Popular on the workshop circuit, Cherry gives lively classes on writing and the writing life. Pulling no punches when asked how to become a published writer, Cherry insists, "Sit your butt in the chair and write. There's no magic to it. Writing is hard work. It isn't for sissies or whiners."

Cherry loves to spend time at home. A corner desk keeps her focused on writing, but the windows behind her, with a panoramic view of the front gardens, are always calling her to come outside and play. Her office has nine-foot ceilings, a fireplace, a television and built-in bookcases that house approximately 3,500 books.

"What can I say? My keeper shelf has been breeding in the middle of the night, rather like dry cleaners' wire clothes hangers."

Where can we find out more about you Cherry Adair?

On my website:

www.CherryAdair.com, Twitter and my beloved Facebook . I love hearing from readers – wherever you may find me.

Look for these thrilling eBooks and print books on the
Cherry Adair Online Bookstore.
http://www.shop.cherryadair.com
CUTTER CAY SERIES
Undertow
Riptide
Vortex
Stormchaser
Hurricane
Whirlpool
FALLEN AGENTS OF T-FLAC Series
Absolute Doubt - Book 1
LODESTONE SERIES
Afterglow
Hush - Book 1
Gideon - Book 2
Relentless
T-FLAC/PSI
Edge of Danger Enhanced
Edge of Fear Enhanced
Edge of Darkness Enhanced
T-FLAC/WRIGHT FAMILY
Kiss and Tell Enhanced
Hide and Seek Enhanced
In Too Deep Enhanced
Out of Sight Enhanced
On Thin Ice Enhanced
T-FLAC/BLACK ROSE
Hot Ice Enhanced
White Heat Enhanced
Ice Cold

NIGHT TRILOGY T-FLAC/PSI
Night Fall
Night Secrets
Night Shadow
T-FLAC SHORT STORIES
Playing for Keeps Enhanced
Ricochet
SHORT STORY
Snowball's Chance T-FLAC/PSI

Paranormal
Dark Prism
Writer's Tool
Cherry Adairs' Writers' Bible
Plotting by Color
Dialog
Character
Connect with Cherry on CherryAdair.com for info on new
releases, access to exclusive offers, and much more!